"You don't ___ thing for me."

Lin's words were rude, but Soren said quite pleasantly, "Let's put that to the test, shall we?"

The next moment he had pulled her against him and her protest was smothered by his lips. He was gentle but extremely thorough, and Lin felt dizzy and breathless when he lifted his mouth from hers.

His lips brushed her temple, murmured a few soft words that it took her a moment to understand.

"Tell me why you came here, Melinda," he was saying. "What were you running away from?"

"What do you mean?" Lin snapped, pushing away from him sharply. "I'm not running away!"

And she wasn't. In fact, she was running *toward* something she had been searching for all her life....

Never Count Tomorrow

by

DAPHNE CLAIR

Harlequin Books

TORONTO • LONDON • LOS ANGELES • AMSTERDAM
SYDNEY • HAMBURG • PARIS • STOCKHOLM • ATHENS • TOKYO

Original hardcover edition published in 1980
by Mills & Boon Limited

ISBN 0-373-02420-7

Harlequin edition published August 1981

CHAPTER ONE

PAIKEA looked like any other small New Zealand town. The few shops that lined the tarsealed main street were a mixture of old style buildings with corrugated iron roofs curving over to shade the footpath, and modern ones in concrete block and shiny tiles. The post office was a smallish wooden building of no recognisable period, and when Lin walked into it the brown polished lino on the floor seemed to intensify the dim contrast with the sunny day outside.

She blinked, and as her eyes adjusted, saw a counter, with a young woman behind it facing a tall man who leaned over, in his hand a piece of paper which he placed on the counter, indicating some figures on it with a jabbing brown finger. His outdoor tan contrasted with the light hair that almost touched his collar.

The girl looked confused and made some hesitant remark, then smiled at the man. The man had his back to Lin, but she could have sworn that the muscles of the broad shoulders suddenly tensed under the light blue shirt, and certainly he shifted his feet so that the heavy boots he wore made an impatient sound on the lino. His voice when he spoke was low, but he sounded as though he was trying —perhaps not very hard—to contain his temper, and she distinctly heard the word 'incompetence' uttered, as it were, through gritted teeth. The girl, who was fair-skinned and quite pretty, blushed hotly, whispered something in an agitated way and disappeared through a doorway, taking the paper with her. Lin was sorry for her.

The man stayed motionless, leaning on the counter, and

Lin looked about the walls at the posters advertising postal services, vaguely hoping to see a map of the district. In a few minutes the girl returned with a middle-aged man wearing glasses and an apologetic look. 'I see there's been an error made,' he said. 'I'm sorry about that, Mr——'

'Never mind.' The interruption was brusque. 'Just get it fixed, will you?'

'Yes, of course, we'll send you an amended account.'

The man said, 'Thanks,' and turned so abruptly that Lin, who was hovering behind him awaiting her turn, instinctively stepped back. It wasn't that she had been so close to him, but when he straightened he seemed very big, tall and broad-shouldered, and altogether too much for the small space.

The brown lino was worn in patches, and her slim high-heeled shoe caught an uneven piece and made her stagger. The man was almost passing her, but he shot out a hand that gripped her arm with bruising force and steadied her.

Her eyes met a hard, sea-green gaze beneath frowning brows that were darker than the streaky blond hair above a wide tanned forehead. His face was striking, rather than handsome, unusually tapered to the chin, but the jut of the chin, the firmness of the mouth, and the width of the cheekbones gave an impression of strength. Perhaps she stared a bit, or perhaps he saw in her wide blue eyes the resentment and indignation she had felt on behalf of the girl clerk when he treated her with such marked impatience. As he slowly released her arm, his eyebrows rose a little, in apparent surprised interrogation. He took a step backwards and surveyed her swiftly from the dark hair that just touched her shoulders, down past the silk shirt and flared skirt in two shades of pink, to her slim legs, neat ankles, and pretty feet in fashion sandals. His gaze lingered there and returned to her face with faint but unmistakable derision. His face plainly said that she was a fool, that her shoes were an idiotic vanity, but that it didn't surprise him. Because she was a woman, she supposed. It appeared that for some reason he didn't have a great deal of time for the species.

As he spun on his heel and strode out, she supposed she should have thanked him. He had quick reflexes, and she might have fallen if he hadn't caught her.

With a tiny shrug, she turned to the girl behind the counter, who had recovered her own poise and was smiling in a friendly way, rather less charmingly than she had at the man, but perhaps that was because she was still a little upset.

'Can you tell me where to find Hokianga Road?' Lin asked her. 'I have a map, but it isn't very detailed——'

She took the map from her bag, and the girl obligingly pointed out the way for her—through the town, and turn at the dairy factory, carry on for a few miles, then turn right. Lin thanked her warmly to make up for the rudeness of her last customer, and went out into the sunshine, to get into her car. Ruefully she looked at the dust that had collected on the red paint, dulling its shine. The car had been bought new quite recently, and she took rather good care of it. Still, it would soon clean, she told herself. What was a bit of dust, after all?

Some ten minutes later, as she crawled up a winding hill road in the wake of a cattle truck which was churning dust behind it thickly enough to almost blind her, she was less sanguine about the stuff. She stuck close behind the truck for some way, hoping for a chance to pass, but the road was growing narrower, and eventually she dropped back to try and escape the choking, gritty cloud. She opened one of the windows that she had closed up to keep the dust out, and eased back the accelerator, then decided she might as well stop until the truck was well out of the way.

As she cut the engine, silence seemed to descend like a cloak on the landscape. That was the immediate impression, although when she listened she could hear quite plainly the whining roar of the truck still climbing, and a bird call or two from the few trees that reared above the manuka scrub growing on each side of the road. She climbed out, walking awkwardly over the stony road to a gap in the manuka where she could look down at the valley below. The farms looked neat and green down there, sleepy in the late spring sun, the low roofs of the farmhouses looking squat from where she stood. In the distance were rolling hills with no glimpse of the sea beyond them, but it was there, not more than twenty miles away. Between the sea that lay gently on its coast to the east, and the mountains that sheltered it from the western winds, the Bay of Plenty was blessed with a balmy climate, she had been told, where it seldom got colder than twenty degrees Fahrenheit, and the humidity that made heat uncomfortable further north was almost missing.

She could no longer hear the truck, the dust on the road had settled, and the air seemed to have a sharp, tangible freshness. There was no haziness in the view before her, and the sky was a clear, brilliant blue, arcing overhead. A skylark rocketed from one of the green paddocks below and hung twittering and twirling above the land, its song coming faintly to her ears as a breeze sprang from nowhere and brought spent white manuka blossom drifting by her to settle softly on the bushes below the road.

Lin shivered and rubbed the sudden gooseflesh from her arms, then returned to the car. A cloud had come seemingly from nowhere and crossed the shining face of the sun and she was suddenly in shadow. She wasn't chilly now, but a nervous shiver made her clench her teeth, and something in her whispered that even now it was not too late to turn back.

She took a deep breath and started the car. Of course it was too late. She wasn't turning back now, not for anything or anybody. She had waited too long for this. And the advertisement, coming out of the blue, had made it seem *meant*, somehow. It couldn't be that she was doing the wrong thing, it just couldn't be.

As she swung the car back on to the road her hand went down to touch her bag on the seat beside her, as if for reassurance. She had cut out the advertisement and kept it, reading it over so many times that before she had summoned up courage to apply for the job, she could have recited it off by heart.

> *Healthy, willing worker wanted to help in house and mind lively pre-school child while mother works on farm. Own room with TV. Weekends off. Good wage. Bay of Plenty. Apply in writing, to R. Wingard, R.D. Paikea.*

Wingard, Paikea. Lin had stared at the name and address for a long time when she first saw the ad in the daily paper. For weeks she had been at a standstill, making impossible plans, discarding them, weaving daydreams, making impulsive resolutions and immediately breaking them. And now here was *R. Wingard, Paikea,* giving her the perfect, *perfect* opportunity, the chance in a million that couldn't be passed up.

Apply in writing. At first her hands had been shaking so much that she had to tear up four letters before she managed a creditable one. And it wasn't easy to decide what to put, either. She couldn't claim any great expertise at either housework or looking after small children. But she did know how to cook a meal; and cleaning house, although she couldn't pretend to love the work, was largely a matter of common sense and elbow grease. In the end she put her age —twenty-three—said she liked children, which was true as far as it went, and enjoyed country life, which was also true; she had spent a couple of holidays on farms as a child, and retained pleasant memories. She said she was strong and healthy and willing to work hard. She had some experience at kitchen work and waitressing, and had also done outdoor seasonal work. That looked good, she thought—no need to mention, unless they asked, that the restaurant job had lasted only the duration of one university holiday, and the apple and grape picking on a working holiday in Australia had nearly killed her at the time. The thought of her aching back and sunburned skin, torn fingernails and scratched hands could still make her wince. But it had been a challenge and in its way enjoyable, even if she had no desire to repeat the experience.

She had debated whether to add a year or two to her age, decided it wasn't necessary, and giggled a little hysterically to herself as she definitely vetoed the idea of mentioning her Arts degree. A knowledge of literature and history was scarcely relevant qualification for the job.

After the letter was posted she waited in an agony of suspense for a reply, and when ten days later the phone rang and a warm voice said, 'Hello, I'm Teresa Wingard— you wrote to us about the job——' she gripped the receiver with sweat-slippery hands and felt her heart thudding as she answered squeakily, 'Yes—yes, I did,' and prayed inwardly, Oh, please, please, God, I've got it, please let her say I've got the job!

Afterwards she tried to put a face to the warm, friendly voice, and failed. Patience, she told herself, patience. They wanted her as soon as possible and she promised eagerly to come at the beginning of the following week. Teresa Wingard told her what the wages would be, and she realised that it might seem odd that she hadn't even asked about what she would be paid. The ad had said 'good wages', but of course that could mean anything.

It had also said there was a 'lively pre-school child' to look after. Translated that might mean 'little monster', she supposed, but that hurdle could be dealt with when she came to it. Surely one small child couldn't be too much for an intelligent, willing, healthy young woman to handle.

Lin slowed as a roadside letterbox came into view, with a long driveway snaking up the rise behind it to a sprawling brick farmhouse. The name on the box was Treasor, and she accelerated again, peering at more boxes along the winding road until she braked rather suddenly at the sight of 'Wingard' printed in bold black letters on a white box. The car had stalled with her hasty stop, and she had to start the engine again to turn into the drive that curved rather attractively through an avenue of young oaks. One day they would be old and gracious and make a lovely tunnel leading to the house.

The drive curved round to a garage set a little to the rear of the house. She stopped on the circular turnaround and looked at the weatherboard dwelling. It was solid-looking and rambled a little, as though it had been added to at some time, perhaps to accommodate a growing family. It was neither interestingly old nor stylishly new, probably built in the thirties, she guessed. But there was a comfortable, homely look about its uneven roof lines and wide veranda, the two open sun porches and the one that had evidently been glassed in at some time to provide an extra room. The paint on the boards and the corrugated iron roof looked fresh and clean, and the lawn that was fenced off around it was freshly mown, although the garden shrubs looked a little untidy and neglected. The open gate to the driveway was painted white, and in good repair.

A dog came scuffling out from behind the garage, gave one short, questioning bark, and approached the car with tail cautiously wagging. Lin stepped out with her hand outstretched for the dog to sniff, and a woman came out of the house calling, 'Remus! Here, boy!'

The dog obediently trotted off, its shaggy tan coat lifting as it moved, and Lin stood clutching the car door and watching the woman walk towards her.

'Hello, I'm Teresa Wingard. You must be Lin.' Her smile matched the warm voice Lin had heard on the phone. As Lin stood motionless, the smile widened a little, though sympathetically. 'Old Remus won't hurt you. You needn't be scared.'

'I'm not scared,' Lin said, but her voice sounded breathless and odd. And it wasn't true, quite. She was terribly nervous, stupidly so. And if she didn't pull herself together pretty quickly, her employer would think she was some kind of nut.

She gave a smile of her own, and tried to think of something sensible to say.

But there was no need. The other woman touched her arm and said, 'You've had a long trip from Auckland—you must be tired. Come in and have a cup of tea. We'll worry about your luggage later.'

She was shown the bathroom, and freshened up while Teresa Wingard put the electric jug on, and when Lin came back to the kitchen feeling a little more in command of herself, the tea was made. She sat down obediently at the table with a crisp cross-stitched cloth on its surface, and watched as cups and saucers and a plateful of home-made biscuits were placed in front of her. She had hardly noticed, outside, what Teresa Wingard looked like, except for the friendly, sympathetic smile. Now she saw a nice-looking woman in her forties, dark-haired like herself, with a few grey wisps in front; when she wasn't smiling her face had a slightly strained look, but the smile lit it up, making her look much younger and prettier. She was quite slim, with a full bustline, and the cotton dress she wore looked a little baggy on her, as though she might have recently lost some weight.

She smiled again now, as she sat down opposite Lin and poured the tea, passing a cup to Lin. 'Drink up,' she said, the blue eyes kind.

'Thank you, Mrs Wingard,' Lin said steadily.

'No need for that. Call me Teresa.'

Lin's hand shook, slopping tea into her saucer, and she dipped her head to hide the dismaying sting of tears. She didn't know it, but her face was pale, and Teresa hadn't missed the trembling of her fingers on the cup.

Using both hands, Lin lifted the cup and carefully sipped at the tea. Teresa looked concerned. 'You *are* tired,' she said. 'Have you had lunch?'

'Yes, I stopped for an hour at Tauranga. I'm all right, really.' Lin managed a trembly smile. 'When I've had another cup of tea, I'll be fine.'

She was, too. The first hurdle was over, after all. From now on there was surely nothing to be worried about.

She said, 'Would you tell me what you will be wanting me to do—what the job entails exactly?'

'Well, housework, mainly. The family make their own beds in the morning and they're supposed to keep their rooms tidy. I'd better tell you who there is in the house, I suppose. We've two daughters, fifteen and sixteen—Susan is sitting for University Entrance this year, her second try, and Tracy for School Certificate. They're hard workers but not brilliant, so I don't want to break into their studies by calling on them for a lot of household chores. They have to spend more than an hour on the school bus before and after school, too, which means they don't have very much time for their homework. Davy is nearly twelve—he's the clever one—and starts at the High School next year. And then there's Scotty—our little afterthought. He's only three. At the moment he's having an afternoon nap. I can't always persuade him to have it, but he had a heavy day yesterday at a friend's birthday party, and he's still getting over it.

'Actually, he's the main reason that we need you,' she explained. 'My husband had an accident about a month ago—a tractor rolled on him, and he was lucky to get out alive. As it was, he broke both legs and crushed his ribs. Thank God there was a safety frame on the machine, or it might have been even worse. Anyway, he needs help on the farm, and we haven't had much success with farm workers in the past, but I can help—I used to before the children came along, and I enjoy milking and caring for the calves and being outside. But Scotty, when he's awake, needs watching every minute—a farm is a dangerous environment for an adventurous little boy, and he seems to have *no* sense of danger. You aren't being employed as a nursemaid, exactly, but when I'm out on the farm Scotty is your first priority—okay?'

'Okay.' Lin's smile was the first really natural one she had managed since her arrival. 'Is your husband in hospital?' she asked.

'No. He's been home since the first week, but his legs are just out of plaster and he's using sticks to get about. He was driven into Paikea today for our own doctor to check him over.'

The door from the kitchen to the passageway that had been standing ajar was crashed open, and a small tornado erupted into the room, leaping in a blur of white underclothes and sleep-pinked baby flesh, on to Teresa's knee.

Teresa laughed, hugging the small boy to her and smoothing tousled dark curls, as the child buried his head in her bosom, swivelling one blue eye to inspect Lin.

'This is Scott,' said Teresa. 'Say hello to Lin, Scotty.'

The eye disappeared, as Scott turned his head further against his mother.

Lin said, 'Hello, Scott.'

His head turned slowly until he could see her, then quickly returned to its former position as he muttered, 'Hello.'

Lin laughed softly, so that he shouldn't hear, and Teresa said cheerfully, 'He won't be shy for long. Excuse us, Lin. I'll put some clothes on the scrap, and then I'll take you to your own room.'

By the time she returned, with Scott dressed in a striped tee-shirt and blue shorts, Lin had washed up the cups and saucers and cleared the table, putting things away carefully in the places she had noted as Teresa got them out. Teresa thanked her, and, using strategy, asked Scott to show Lin her room.

He looked at the stranger consideringly and then nodded abruptly and trotted off down the wide passageway, leaving her to follow.

The room seemed to be an addition. It was at the side of the house, where it would catch the morning sun, and the covered-in porch she had noticed opened off it, making a bright, charming little annexe furnished with a reclining chair, a low table and a set of bookshelves. The main room was large, and had a bed, a big wardrobe, a dressing table with several drawers and a low easy chair as well as the television set tucked into a corner. The bed was unfashionably high but looked comfortable, and when she peeped beneath the sheets she found it had a foam rubber

mattress. There was no luxury, but ample comfort, and
Teresa, coming to the door, said, 'If there's anything you
need, Lin, just ask. The bathroom is just along here——'
she pointed down the passageway to where it turned a
corner. 'This one is mainly used by the girls. There's another bathroom at the back of the house, and Ray and I
had a little washroom built into our bedroom last year.'

Scott suddenly grabbed at Lin's hand. 'See *my* room!'
he demanded.

'That would be nice,' Lin smiled, and saw Teresa's face
relax. Obviously it was important that Scott should take to
her, and she could see that his mother was relieved at the
friendly overture.

She admired the brilliant orange bedspread with the
appliquéd fluffy teddy bear in the middle, taking him up
on his invitation to stroke Teddy, and made complimentary
remarks about the pictures of trains, rocket ships and animals that were pinned on the walls. When Scott suddenly
lost interest in her and dropped to the floor to start running
a plastic train about the pattern of the bright rag rug on the
floor, she smiled at Teresa's apologetic raising of eyes, and
accompanied her out into the hall.

'The others all ended up quite civilised,' Teresa said
hopefully, and Lin laughed and asked if she could see the
rest of the house.

It all had the same air of relaxed comfort, and she didn't
think there would be too much bother in keeping it that
way. And little Scott had touched her heart already. She
had no doubt he could be a handful to manage, but he had
accepted her, and she would learn from his mother the best
ways to cope with him.

She suggested bringing in her cases, but Teresa said,
'Leave them, if you don't want anything urgently. Soren
will bring them in for you when he brings Ray back from

the doctor's. They shouldn't be long. I gave them a bit of shopping to do, if Ray was feeling up to it, but I don't think they'll stay in town longer than they have to.'

The girls and Davy came in from school first, though, and were introduced. Susan was tanned and freckled, with short sandy curls and a wide smile and a bouncy manner. Tracy, a year younger, was darker and more like her mother, although her eyes were hazel. She was pretty and just a tiny bit plump, which evidently caused her some anguish, for she ate one of her mother's fresh biscuits with a martyred air, bewailing her own lack of will power and her mother's apparent cruelty in putting temptation in her way.

Teresa said briskly, 'Nonsense. You're not fat, my girl.' And Davy, dark and blue-eyed like his younger brother, said unfeelingly, 'You should get more exercise. That'd stop you getting fat.'

'I get enough, *junior*!' his sister retorted. But the teasing and the grimaces they made at each other were quite unmalicious, and both were grinning as Davy dodged a mock blow that Tracy aimed at him.

A car drew up outside, and Teresa said, 'That'll be Soren and Ray.'

Lin hadn't asked who Soren was; evidently he wasn't one of the family, probably a neighbour from one of the other farms. Davy darted out to meet his father, and the girls gathered up their schoolbags and left in the direction of the room they shared close to hers. Teresa went and stood in the kitchen doorway, and as Lin gathered up milky glasses and wiped crumbs from the table, she heard a deep voice assuring Teresa that everything was coming along just as it should, according to the doctor.

Lin turned from the sink as Teresa stepped back and the two men came into the kitchen, one leaning on a stick and supported on the other side by a man she instantly recognised, with a faint shock of dismay. It was the man from the post office encounter. She got over it quickly— he was obviously a local, and there was no reason he shouldn't be a neighbour of the Wingards, maybe even a good one. He was busy helping Mr Wingard to sit down in one of the kitchen chairs, and hadn't yet noticed her presence in the room. When he did, as he straightened, he stared a little, his green eyes suddenly narrowing as though it didn't please him much to find her here.

Teresa said, 'Ray, this is Lin. She arrived about an hour ago. And Lin——' she turned to the tall fair man standing with one hand on the back of her husband's chair, and the other hooked into the belt of his fitting trousers, '—this is Soren, our eldest son.'

Their son! For long moments, Lin was completely disorientated. She felt as though the floor beneath her feet had suddenly receded, leaving her standing on a void, and the room tipped a little and then righted itself. *Their son?* But it wasn't possible, she knew it wasn't possible. The man must be at least thirty ... Had she, after all, made a terrible mistake?

She repeated it aloud, her voice high with disbelief. 'Your son? But—he can't be!'

She saw the quick frown between his brows, the angry darkening of the green eyes, and without even looking she knew that the hand on the chairback had tightened ominously. She looked away from him, in desperation, her wide eyes finding Teresa's, looking for reassurance. 'You're not old enough——' she said. 'Are you?'

Soren hadn't taken his eyes from her face. She knew it. And she knew, as though he had shouted it at her, that he was hating her. The force of it was coming at her in tangible waves. She kept determinedly looking at Teresa, who was exchanging a surprised, rather amused look with her husband. But it was Soren who answered Lin, his voice flat, but with a hint of harshness he had used to the girl in the post office. 'You're quick,' he said. 'Actually, Mrs Wingard is my stepmother.'

'We never think about it,' said Teresa. Her glance at her stepson was a little anxious. Then she smiled at Lin. 'Most people don't seem to realise it, but I would have been thirteen when Soren was born. I'm flattered that you realised I was a bit young to be his mother.'

Soren shifted his eyes at last from Lin, and looked curiously at Teresa. 'Does it bother you?' he asked. 'I never thought about it before, but it must be a bit annoying if people assume you're older than you are, because you apparently have a great hulking son like me.'

'Of course it doesn't bother me, Soren. Don't be silly! I've always been terribly proud of my big son. By the way, we have a job for a strong man. Lin's cases are still in her car. Would you get them out for her and take them into her room?'

'Sure,' he said, after a moment. 'Right now.'

He went out, and Lin had the distinct feeling that he was glad to get away from them all for a few minutes. Then she remembered the trunk of the car was locked. 'My keys——' she said, darting for her bedroom. 'I'll get them.'

When she dashed outside with the keys in her hand, he was just closing the car door. He watched her coming, and said, 'I thought you might have left them in the ignition. Don't do it round here, will you? Young Scott might decide to go for a drive.'

'I never do,' she answered. 'It isn't safe to leave them, in Auckland.'

She unlocked the trunk, and he came beside her and grasped the handles of her cases, a matching pair in blue leather. Swinging them out, he commented. 'You're a city girl, then.'

His voice was casual, but his quick glance had been sharply inquisitive.

Cautiously she said, 'I have been lately.' She took out the holdall and the round pigskin make-up bag that made up the remainder of her luggage, and locked the trunk up again while he stood by, waiting for her, then he stepped back to allow her to precede him into the house.

In her room he put the cases on the floor by the bed, and for a moment or two stood looking down at them thoughtfully.

Lin said, 'Thank you, Mr Wingard.'

'Soren,' he said. 'What's Lin short for? Lynette?'

'Melinda,' she said. 'I don't use my full name.'

'Why not? It suits you.'

She looked up at him and saw that it was hardly a compliment. His eyes held derision and a faint, bored contempt. 'Melinda' sounded like a silly, pretty little nitwit, she had always thought. He shared her opinion and he thought the name suited her.

Resentment stirred in her. Ever since she had seen him walk in the door, his arm supporting his father, she had been uneasy and—yes, frightened. He had completely dispelled the atmosphere of safety and comfort and ease that she had breathed from the moment she entered this house. As soon as his green eyes found hers in the kitchen, the air had begun crackling with the tension between them. It wasn't just that he didn't like women in general, although she suspected that was part of it. That wave of hostility had been directed at *her* personally.

She had never been hated before. She wasn't sure if she had ever been really loved, but no one had hated her.

She said, 'Soren is an unusual name. Is it Scandinavian?'

Something happened in his face, although the expression remained the same. It was just as if an invisible film of ice had descended over his features. 'I believe it is,' he said.

Ray Wingard was sandy-haired, his open face very like his eldest daughter's. There was nothing remotely Scandinavian about either of them. The Viking ancestry that showed in Soren's wide cheekbones beneath the tanned skin, the eyes the colour of a chilly northern fiord, had not come from Ray Wingard. She didn't quite dare ask about his mother, but her eyes played thoughtfully over his face, and she said, 'You're not at all like your father, are you?'

Her voice was light and chatty, just making small talk, but she hadn't intended him to be fooled, and he wasn't.

'Not a bit,' he said flatly. And it sounded like a threat. Then he walked out, leaving her standing there.

Lin took a deep breath, wondering how on earth it had happened—the quick antagonism, the sharp awareness that here was an enemy, and a dangerous one.

She shook her head sharply. Now that he was gone she could tell herself she must be imagining things. She was strung up, tense, ready to read into people's words and actions all kinds of things that weren't there. Soren hadn't fallen at her feet, but few men did. One or two had taken a tumble, because she was quite attractive, and she hadn't been above being flattered by such admiration, but there had been nothing serious. But Soren couldn't have hated her on sight—it was too unreasonable. She *wouldn't* believe it.

CHAPTER TWO

IT was getting on towards four o'clock, and Lin had a feeling that was milking time, so she left her cases where Soren had put them, and returned to the kitchen. Ray wasn't there any more, but Teresa was peeling potatoes on to a piece of newspaper with quick, expert movements, and dropping them into the sink.

Soren had been standing talking to Teresa, but as Lin came through the door from the passage, he began to move without haste towards the outer one leading to the back porch and the 'muckroom' where gumboots and overalls were kept.

Lin said, 'I'll do that. Are you milking today—Teresa?'

The older woman turned with a smile. 'Davy can help Soren today,' she said. 'You're tired, Lin. Go and talk to Ray in the sitting room—keep him company.'

Soren had stopped in the doorway and turned. Ignoring him, Lin said, 'I'm not tired any more, honestly. All I needed was a cup of tea. Now that I'm here I might as well start working.'

'Start tomorrow,' said Teresa. 'You'll be fresh, then.' She looked at Lin appraisingly. 'You are looking better, but I don't mind telling you I was quite worried about you at first. You looked quite white, for a while. I do think you should take it easy for tonight.'

From the corner of her eye Lin caught Soren's impatient movement.

'At least let me help——' she began, when he interrupted.

'For heaven's sake, Ma, let her do what she's being paid for,' he exclaimed. 'We didn't hire you a home help so that you could spend your time nursing the girl! You've enough on your hands already.'

Teresa turned in astonishment. 'Soren!'

Lin looked at him, too, and saw the quick apology in his eyes, for his stepmother, not for her.

'He's right,' she said swiftly. 'It's my job.'

But Teresa wouldn't have it. 'Not today, it isn't,' she said firmly. 'You can manage without me for one more day, Soren——'

'It isn't that——' he began impatiently, but she over-rode him.

'You didn't see this poor girl when she arrived—it's a long, tiring drive from Auckland, and I won't be a slave-driver. Tonight she's a guest, and tomorrow she can start work. Now, you go and milk those cows. Davy's bringing them in for you.'

He went out, not with a good grace, and Lin said, '*Ma*—is that what he calls you?'

Teresa laughed. 'Yes—it began as a sort of joke. At least, he pretended it was. Oh, it's a long story, you don't want to hear our family history.'

Don't I, though? thought Lin, curbing the urge to ask for it right now. She had only just arrived, after all. No one was going to tell her their life story tonight. She said, 'Tell me what I can do.'

In mock exasperation, Teresa exclaimed, 'Heavens! You're almost as stubborn as Soren. You know where the sitting room is. Go and keep Ray company, there's a good girl. He'll be glad of someone new to talk to.'

He was reading the paper when she walked into the room, but he looked up and put it away when she sat down and told him what her orders were. 'I thought I should be helping,' she said. 'And so did Soren. But Teresa—Mrs Wingard—said I'm to start tomorrow.'

'I'm sure she won't mind if you call her Teresa, Lin.'

'She asked me to,' Lin admitted.

'Good. And I'm Ray. We want you to be one of the family, you know.'

'Thank you.' She couldn't trust herself to say any more, but she hoped he knew she meant it.

He shifted in his chair, and she asked, 'Are you in pain? Teresa told me about the accident.'

'Just a bit stiff,' he said. 'I was lucky, really. Could have been a lot worse. Soren got me out.'

'He was there?'

'Luckily for me. I might have been lying there for hours pinned under the tractor, otherwise. It's happened to other people. I was pretty scared, as a matter of fact. But my boy——' he looked away suddenly and cleared his throat. '—well, he worked like a demon, getting me out. He had to lever it off me, you see, first. He ripped battens from the fence with his bare hands, and shifted rocks it would take two men to lift. I've never seen anything like it.'

'Adrenalin,' Lin murmured.

'That's what he said. It comes to the rescue in emergencies, he reckons. All I can say is, I know who came to *my* rescue, and I'm proud of him.'

That was natural, she supposed. Teresa had said that, too—that she was proud of her big son. But he wasn't hers, not hers by birth, anyway. She loved him as her own, that was obvious. Soren was fortunate in that. Did he realise how fortunate he was? Lin wondered, and felt an odd, stirring anger mingled with a deep, familiar pain.

Scott wandered into the room holding a battered toy bulldozer, which he presented to his father with a long monologue that Lin entirely failed to follow. Ray's answers were noncommittal, but apparently satisfactory, and after a while his son climbed up on his knee and turned to stare at Lin. She smiled, and he turned his head into his father's shoulder. Ray laughed and tousled his son's hair with a big hand. 'You'll have your work cut out with this one,' he told her. 'Know much about kids?'

One thing she had learned already about this family. You couldn't lie to them. So what could she say now? 'Not a lot,' would be close to the truth. 'Practically nothing' might be even closer. But it would hardly increase Ray Wingard's respect for her ability. She said, 'They're people, aren't they?'

Thank heaven Soren wasn't here—he would have looked down his Viking nose at her inanity, for sure. But Ray threw back his head and laughed, then said, 'You'll do!' which seemed to denote approval, anyway. Even though he did add, a minute later, 'Sometimes I wonder, though——' and the implication seemed to be, *You'll learn*.

No doubt she would, but she didn't think it was going to be so terribly hard.

Soren stayed for tea at the big table in the dining room, that Lin gathered was used only for the evening meal, the formica one in the kitchen being adequate for breakfast and lunch. She gathered that Soren didn't live in the house, but in a cottage on the farm that was supposed to house a farm worker. Presumably he would be eating here every evening. She would get used to it. He still—disturbed her, even though he scarcely glanced her way. With everyone else she felt instantly at home, but not with Soren. He was an outsider—no, she realised painfully, *she* was the outsider. But if it hadn't been for him, she wouldn't have felt like one at all. Everyone else went out of their way to make her feel welcome and draw her into the magic circle of their mutual affection. But not Soren. When he did look at her, his eyes were cool as a winter sea. And there was no friendliness in his smile when he said goodnight. It was sharp and seemed to hold speculation and a not very kind amusement. 'I'll see you tomorrow, Melinda,' he said. And as if he had accused her of shirking, she thought, If you do, I'll be working fit to break my neck, don't you worry!

She worked harder than anyone expected or demanded of her, cleaning, polishing and scrubbing in that first week until Teresa protested that the place had never been so spick and span in its life. Not that it needed so much, but Lin had an obsession—no one would be able to say she didn't earn the good wage she was getting for this!

Ray kept Scott occupied most of the time while Teresa was at the milking shed or on the farm, but Ray couldn't run after a child if Scott should suddenly decide to take off somewhere, so Lin stayed within earshot. She didn't get up as early as the milkers, but made them a hearty breakfast each morning, and cooked for the family tea in the evening. Her nails broke and she cut their prettily oval shape back to a sensible length, and used lots of scented cream on her hands, but they showed the results of an unaccustomed amount of hot water and detergents and potato-peeling, for all that.

On Friday night she didn't set her alarm clock, and the following morning slept blissfully on until nearly eleven, emerging from her room just in time for a sandwich lunch prepared by Susan and Tracy.

'What are you going to do with your day off?' Tracy asked her. 'Do you have any friends round here?'

'Not yet. I thought I'd like to take a walk around the farm this afternoon. If that's all right?' She glanced at Ray.

'Sure,' he said. 'Want someone to show you round?'

Soren was leaning against the bench, a sandwich in one

hand and mug of tea in the other. Surprisingly, he said, 'I will. What time can you be ready, Melinda?'

He always called her Melinda, the only one who did so. Susan and Tracy had said, 'That's pretty!' but they called her Lin.

She said, 'I don't need a guide—do I? If you're busy——'

'Soren will take you,' said Ray. 'He'll be able to explain things to you, and make it more interesting. And he'll keep you out of the way of the bulls. You wouldn't want to get across one of them.'

She certainly wouldn't, so she accepted Soren's escort, mustering a smile and a pretty thank you for him.

He didn't appear to appreciate either, merely nodding in a bored way. She asked, 'Will I need boots?'

'No,' Soren told her. 'Sneakers or a pair of sensible shoes will do. The ground's dry at this time of the year.'

Lin was wearing jeans and a shirt, and didn't keep him waiting long while she changed her sandals for a pair of canvas sneakers and tied the sleeves of a light jersey loosely about her throat.

Soren was wearing jeans, too, with a faded plaid cotton shirt open half way down the front. He pulled on his boots at the back door, and asked, 'Do you want to see the milking shed?'

'Is it interesting?'

He looked at her consideringly and said, 'That depends on what you'd call interesting. It's fairly new and fairly fancy as milking sheds go.'

Lin tried another smile. 'It sounds interesting.'

He didn't smile back, but kept looking at her a moment longer, then said, 'Okay. Let's go.'

She decided it was definitely the fanciest milking shed she had ever seen, although admittedly her experience wasn't great. The smell of disinfectant mingled with the usual cow smells, and there was a lot of concrete, all designed with slopes to drainage outlets so that cleaning down was made easy and efficient. The milking stand was a revolving one, so that the cows walked easily into the bails and easily out again when they had been relieved of their milk, and more animals could be milked by fewer people than in a conventional shed. There was a special concrete and tile room for utensils and cleaning gear, and a small office for keeping records. The stainless steel vat where the milk was chilled and awaited collection by tanker was standard, mounted in a concrete bay a few feet above the ground. Soren sprang down lightly and turned, his hands on Lin's waist lifting her down beside him before she realised what he was about to do. He let her go as soon as she got her balance, and led the way round the shed to the cattle race which the cows used on their way into the shed. Of course, there were cowpats there, and she thought he grinned a little as she carefully walked round the fresh ones. But when she looked directly at him, his gaze was fixed ahead and his mouth was straight and firm.

They passed a well-fenced enclosure where a huge, sullen-looking bull stood with lowered head, glaring at them with apparent animosity. 'That's Caesar,' said Soren. 'Not quite as fierce as he looks, but it doesn't pay to take chances.'

'I wouldn't,' she murmured. 'I suppose the *cows* find him attractive.'

Soren gave a short, surprised laugh. 'They don't need to, these days. It's all done with test tubes. Much more efficient than leaving it to nature and the fickleness of females.'

'Oh, Poor Caesar!'

This time the laugh was less surprised, but deep-throated and real. When he looked down at her, still grinning enjoyment, his face looked entirely different, so that her heart did an odd little flip in sheer astonishment. 'Not "poor cows"?' he queried, teasing.

Lin felt the colour run under the skin of her cheeks, and turned away to walk on with her head high. 'Anyway, it isn't only females who are fickle,' she said.

'Did I say that?' he asked, catching up with her.

'You implied it.'

'A figure of speech, Melinda. Don't be so touchy.'

Lin wondered if she was touchy where Soren was concerned. She still had the distinct feeling that he didn't like her, although the overt hostility of their first encounters had abated. She turned to look at him suspiciously and found him regarding her with an expression that was becoming familiar. He often looked at her like that, his eyes coolly watchful and searching, as though he was waiting for her to put a foot wrong somehow.

'Why do you look at me like that?' she demanded.

He looked amused. 'You're very nice to look at. I can't be the first man to tell you so.'

He wasn't, but from him it shocked her for a second or two. She had to adjust her thinking. The other Wingards might have accepted her as an addition to their family, but Soren never had. Certainly he was no kind of big brother to her.

Soren was opening a wooden gate to let them through into a paddock where the cows were grazing. Lin went by him and waited while he closed the gate. 'They're not Jersey cows, are they?' she asked him, taking the opportunity to change the subject.

'No,' he said. 'Mostly Friesians, but some are a Friesian–Jersey cross. Very few people run a pure Jersey herd these days, they were good for cream in the days when butter was the important product. Now skim milk is just as important

for casein, and whole milk is made into powder for overseas markets. The main factor is overall yield, instead of
fat content, so most farmers have switched to other breeds,
or cross-breeds, instead of the Jerseys.'

He went on telling her about the various breeding programmes that were being conducted on this and other
farms, both for dairying and beef purposes, and the at-
tempts to produce strains that would combine the qualities
of good milkers and good beef stock. They had to climb
over a fence at the other side of the paddock, Lin declining
his help and managing to negotiate the barbed wire at the
corner post quite creditably. She was surprised to see
polled beef cattle on the slopes of the hill they were approaching, and said, 'I thought this was a dairy farm.'

'We run beef cattle on the steeper bits,' Soren told her.
'And a few sheep as well. It's a mixed stock farm, but I'm
trying to persuade my father to throw in the dairy herd and
buy more beefers. Come and see this fellow,' he added,
moving to another fence, and pointing out an enormous
cream bull, with massive shoulders, short, enormously
thick legs, and a mass of curls about its handsome head.
'Know what he is?'

Nonplussed, Lin shook her head.

'A Brahman, imported from the East. There aren't too
many of them about. My father hopes he's going to im-
prove our beef stock, and cross-breeding might develop
some interesting strains, perhaps dairy cows that will milk
well and also stand up to tropical conditions better than
most.'

'He's better looking than Caesar, anyway,' she said. 'And
he doesn't seem so fierce.'

The bull ambled over to the fence, and Soren stretched
out a casual hand and scratched at the curls behind the
creature's ear. 'Siddharta here is a pretty gentle fellow,' he

said. 'But keep clear of him, just the same. All bulls are unpredictable.'

They walked again, climbing quite steeply, and Soren slowed to allow Lin to keep up with him. At the top of the hill was a patch of trees, puriri, totara and kohekohe, a heap of tumbled grey rock just below it. It was steep there, and Soren took her hand and pulled her over the last bit with him, until they sank down in the shade of the trees.

He was still holding her hand, and when she made to withdraw it his fingers tightened on hers. Lin looked up at him indignantly, but he was staring down at her hand, turning it over and running his thumb over the slight blisters on her palm, and inspecting the little burn mark across her knuckles. She pulled away strongly, and he let her go, but his eyes on her face were keen for a few moments before he turned away to look at the view before them.

It was quite lovely, a foreground of neatly divided green paddocks holding the scattered herds of cattle and sheep, with the farmhouse on the flat surrounded by trees and shrubs and its white-painted fence. The road disappeared into the manuka and reappeared further down the valley between other lush paddocks, and a narrow river wound its lazy way across the valley floor, darkened by occasional patches of trees. In the distance a range of grey-blue hills hid the sea from sight, but in one place where they dipped quite sharply a glimpse of blue water lay against the slightly paler blue of the sky.

'I didn't realise we were so high up,' Lin murmured.

'Like it?'

'Yes—it's beautiful. Have you always lived here?'

'I was born here. I've lived in other places, but there's always been this to come back to when I wanted it.'

'You're lucky,' she commented.

'Yes. Do you have a home to go back to, Melinda?'

Her hesitation was brief but telling. 'Of course.'

'Parents—brothers and sisters?' he asked.

She resented the question, and didn't want to answer him, but he might be suspicious if she didn't. Carefully she said, 'My mother died when I was nine. I went to live with an aunt who had two children of her own, and when I was thirteen I was sent to boarding school. A very good boarding school,' she added.

He cast a brief, sharp glance at her and said, 'And your father—what was he doing all this time?'

Making money, she thought bitterly. But that was not fair. He had never neglected her; it was true that he couldn't have coped with bringing up a girl child alone, and his almost fanatical preoccupation with business that she had naturally resented might have stemmed from a need to overcome his own grief at the loss of his wife.

'He visited me once a month, usually,' she said. And gave me lots of presents, she almost added, but caution intervened. If Soren guessed that her father was more than well off, he would rather naturally begin to wonder about her taking on a job as a farm housekeeper.

To divert his attention she pointed to a building half hidden by trees some little way from the house below them. 'What's that?' she asked him.

'My home at the moment, such as it is,' he said. 'I'll show it to you when we go down again.'

He had said he had lived in other places, and she would have liked to ask him about them, but curiosity on her part would give him some licence to enquire about her own life. Instead she asked, 'How long have you been working for your father?'

There was a small silence before Soren leaned back in the grass, cradling his fair head in his hands, and said, 'All my life, off and on.'

That didn't tell her much. His tone was almost too casual, and she wondered briefly if he was as reluctant as herself to reveal details of his life. 'Do you like it?' she asked. 'Farm work?'

Again there was that brief hesitation as though he was deciding how to answer. 'It's very satisfying,' he said. 'Being close to the land, watching things grow, working with animals and the fruits of the soil.'

It sounded like something out of a school vocational guidance booklet, and Lin glanced round at him with some suspicion. His eyes were closed, and she couldn't tell if he had been serious or not. Determined to find out, she asked, 'Is that what you really feel?'

After a moment he opened his eyes and looked at her. 'Why not? Don't I strike you as a salt-of-the-earth type?'

Lin could almost have laughed at that. 'Since you ask, no!' she told him baldly.

His mouth curved in a faint grin, and he closed his eyes again. She felt like throwing something at him, so frustrated that she clenched her hands on her raised knees and gritted her teeth.

'Relax,' he said drawlingly, as though her angry tension had communicated itself to him. 'Have a rest before the long walk back.'

'It's not so far,' she said. 'I'm going to explore the trees. It's safe enough, isn't it?'

'Perfectly.' He didn't even open his eyes as she got up and left him, to walk into the cool dimness overhung by deep green leaves. Dry, discarded ones crackled softly under her feet, but beneath them the forest floor was spongy and dark. The dampish aroma of the bush was quite strong with the sun blotted out by the close growth of the trees, and somewhere the clear notes of a bellbird's song chimed into the stillness. She couldn't pick out the author of the song, but a plump native pigeon whirred across her vision in a brief flurry of cerise and white to perch half hidden in the fork of a totara.

Lin found a starry spray of clematis just within touching distance on the end of a puriri branch, and managed to break off one of the flowers. It was one of the last of the season, but was perfect, whitely petalled with deep golden stamens in the centre. She tucked it into her hair behind her ear and reluctantly retraced her steps.

Soren was standing up, leaning against one of the trees at the edge of the bush, and watching for her. He didn't comment on the flower in her dark hair, but she saw his quick eyes taking it in as she came towards him.

'I didn't get lost,' she said.

'I wouldn't have let you go if I'd thought you would. Ready to go?'

'Yes,' she said. She wondered if she had been too long, because he seemed a little irritated. 'I'm sorry if I kept you waiting.'

'There's no hurry,' he shrugged, but he started off down the hill at a pace that made her breathless before they reached the bottom.

Soren seemed to realise it, and though he didn't comment, he slowed his pace considerably for the rest of the way. He didn't speak very much, only answering her questions when she asked about something, and when they reached the cottage she had seen from the top of the hill, she was surprised when he said, 'Here we are—come in,' and opened the unlocked door for her.

He was standing back, waiting for her to take up his invitation. In fact, he seemed to take it for granted that she would. She glanced at him hesitantly, and he said softly, 'Come into my parlour, Melinda.'

She stepped past him, then, into a small room which evidently was the sitting room. At the other end she could see a kitchen through an open door, and another door was ajar to show a glimpse of a neatly made bed with a striped cotton cover.

'Sit down,' invited Soren, indicating the three-piece suite, two deep chairs upholstered in dark soft velvet, and a wide high-backed sofa to match. They looked a little incongruous, but very comfortable. The chair she chose confirmed its appearance as she sank into its embrace.

'Tea, beer, or a soft drink?' Soren asked her, closing the door as he came into the room.

'A soft drink, please,' she said. 'Lemonade, if you have it.'

He went through to the kitchen, and she looked about, seeing the room was basically spartan, with no pictures on the walls, but there was a large round coffee table standing on the slightly worn carpet square, and on the table stood a dark teakwood carving of a crouching leopard, teeth bared, the skin above them wrinkled back in a snarl, the tensile muscles of its shoulders and haunches visible in the smooth wood.

When Soren came back with two glasses of lemonade and put them on the low table, she was gently stroking the carving with one finger.

'Where did you get it?' she asked.

'Sarawak,' he said.

'What were you doing there?' She picked up her glass and leaned back, looking at him as he sat down on the sofa opposite.

'Working.'

'Oh, I *see*!' she said. Of course she didn't, and he laughed reluctantly. 'Why are you being so secretive?' she asked.

Soren looked surprised. 'Secretive?'

'You don't want to tell me anything about yourself, do you?'

'I'm not the only one, then, am I?'

She had fallen right into that, she realised.

'Am I?' he repeated, watching her. Her glance fell to the carved leopard, and she thought, he's like that—tensed and waiting to pounce. She could feel it from across the table between them. This was probably why he had offered to show her round the farm, so that he could take her off guard.

But wasn't she being over-sensitive? He had no reason to suspect her of anything underhand.

She said, 'I don't know what you mean. I answered your questions.'

He put his glass down on the table, and stayed leaning forward, his forearms resting on his thighs. 'Will you answer some more?' he asked.

Warily she said, 'That depends on what they are. Will you?'

He looked at her intently for a moment longer, then leaned back again and said, 'Be my guest.'

Lin didn't know where to start, now. But it would give her a breathing space. And didn't most men enjoy talking about themselves? She said, 'What were you doing in Sarawak?'

'Helping a village to set up an efficient dairy farming industry. I was there for a year—four years ago, now.'

'You were some sort of adviser?'

'Clever girl! I'm attached to the Department of Scientific and Industrial Research. The New Zealand Government sends advisers to various countries under trade and aid agreements to give them the benefit of our experience. As a single man with some useful qualifications and experience, I get that sort of assignment quite often.'

'You said you'd lived in other places,' she said. 'Where else have you been?'

'New Guinea, Thailand, and for short spells in other parts of Asia.'

'It sounds like an interesting job.'

'It is.'

'Are you on holiday now?' she asked.

'No, I'd just returned from a stint in the Philippines when my father had the accident. I have to write up a report of what I've been doing, in detail, and make recommendations for future development. I brought the paperwork here so that I can help out on the farm at the same time. If Dad isn't on his feet when the report's finished, I'll take some leave that's owing, as well.'

'Tell me about the Philippines,' she invited.

He told her, making it vivid and interesting for her, and then about some of the other places he had seen as well. Lin listened and laughed and almost relaxed, but when he seemed to be running out of stories of his travels and adventures, she glanced at her watch and exclaimed, 'Heavens! Is that the time? I must be getting back—thanks for the drink and the talk, Soren. And for showing me the farm.'

She stood up, but he was standing too, between her and the door. 'What's the hurry?' he asked.

'I've taken up enough of your time.'

'What are you frightened of?'

Lin trembled, but stood her ground. 'I'm not frightened,' she said. 'Why should I be?'

'That's what I'd like to know.'

She stared at him, and tried to laugh. 'This conversation is getting nowhere.'

'Agreed. Why don't we just sit down and start again?'

She hesitated. His eyes looked watchful and enigmatic, and she said, 'I—I don't think so. Some other time, perhaps.'

She made to move past him, quite casually, but he put out his hand and held her arm, pushing her firmly on to the sofa. He sat down beside her, with his arm along the back, and turned until he was half facing her. He wasn't touching her at all now, but she had a definite impression that if she moved he would hold her physically right there.

Angrily, she said, 'You're a bit rough, aren't you?'

His brows rose. 'Rough? I haven't hurt you.'

'You disliked me from the start, didn't you?' she burst out. 'You hated me on sight!'

A frown darkened his eyes. 'What gave you that idea?'

'I—felt it,' she said. 'The very first day. You glared at me the minute I opened my mouth.'

Soren's eyes searched her face, then he gave a rueful shrug of his shoulders and ran a hand briefly into his hair, and brought his fist down softly on the sofa back. 'I admit,' he said finally, 'that you touched a nerve—something that goes way back, but you weren't to know, and I haven't been holding it against you, I promise.'

Lin stared. 'How? What did I——?'

Impatiently he said, 'Forget it. Just something you said.'

She had said that Teresa was too young to be his mother. She remembered, and Soren saw her remembering and his face went rigid. She wondered how old he had been when his father married Teresa. About ten, probably. Did he remember his own mother? But obviously it wouldn't do to ask him. She knew he was fond of his stepmother; she could imagine that once he gave her his love, he wouldn't like being reminded that she wasn't his mother.

'I'm sorry,' she said.

'It doesn't matter.'

'I think it does. You still resent it. I can feel it in the air whenever I'm near you.'

Soren looked at her with an odd interest in his eyes. 'What do you feel?'

'Oh—I don't know. Tension—anger. *Something!*'

'You've got your signals confused.' He sounded grimly amused now. 'Hasn't it occurred to you that there's another very common reason for tension between a man and a woman?'

Startled, Lin met his eyes with a sense of shock. 'But there's nothing like that—between you and me!'

'Isn't there?'

She couldn't drag her eyes from his, and suddenly her breath felt oddly strangled, her heartbeats much too fast. His sea-green gaze touched her face with a curious intimacy, and settled on her mouth as her lips parted slightly in trepidation. In a fierce whisper she said, 'Stop it!'

His mouth curved in an unkind smile. 'I haven't done anything,' he said tauntingly.

'You *know* what I mean—you're deliberately trying to——'

He was trying to make her aware of him in a sexual way —she knew it but faltered at putting it into words.

She exclaimed, 'You don't even *like* me!'

'So——?' he drawled, as though that had nothing to do with it.

Lin shook her head in an angry, puzzled little gesture, and he said, 'Tell me why you came here, Melinda. What's the attraction for a girl like you, doing domestic work in a fairly remote farmhouse?'

It took her a moment to adjust, but at least he was off the more disturbing subject of the reasons for their tenseness with each other.

'I needed a job,' she said. 'They're not too easy to get, these days. And I like farm life.'

'You're not accustomed to it, though.'

'How would you know?'

'You know very little about farming, that's very obvious. And what's more, you're not used to doing manual work for your living. *Have* you been used to earning a living, I wonder?'

'If it's any of your business, ask your father for the letter I wrote in answer to his advertisement. Of course I'm used to earning a living—what do you think?'

'I think there's a good deal you didn't put in that letter— which I've seen, by the way. You're not what your letter led us to believe.'

'What are you accusing me of?' she demanded. 'Everything in that letter was the truth.'

'But not the whole truth, I think.' He suddenly took one of her hands in his. 'When you arrived I noticed your hands—pretty pink nails and soft skin. It was a long time since they'd picked fruit, if ever, and you didn't keep them like that doing kitchen work in a restaurant, either. The only two jobs you mentioned . . .'

'I have done other work, but it wasn't relevant. I've been doing—office work, for a while.'

'Why did you leave?'

'I wanted a change.' Lin pulled at her hand, but he still held it.

'So you didn't *need* a job.'

She thought fast. 'Yes, I did. Once I'd left the office job——'

'You mean you resigned before you'd got another job?'

'Yes!'

'Even though jobs are hard to come by?'

His questions were fast, rapped out while his eyes stayed hard on her face.

'What *is* this?' she demanded shrilly. 'The third degree?'

'What have you got to hide?'

'Nothing! I was out of a job, this came up, and it sounded attractive. It's well paid——'

'Ah, yes.'

'Why do you say it like that?' Lin asked.

'You didn't even ask what the pay was, did you?'

'I would have. The advertisement said the wages were good.'

'You can't be that simple. All ads say that, or imply it. The other applicants for the job wanted to know first off what the pay was going to be like.'

'How many applicants were there?'

Soren smiled. 'We weren't besieged. A couple of desperate solo mothers and one girl about to become one.'

Her voice challenging, she said, 'You have something against solo mothers?'

His brows rose a little. 'Not specially. But the idea was for someone to help Ma; not to provide her with another responsibility or an extra child or two to fuss over. Which is why I wasn't too thrilled to see *you*.'

'I don't understand—you knew nothing about me.'

'I was expecting a fit, sensible young person with some experience of hard work——'

'Which you got!' she said swiftly.

'Rubbish! You were so tired by the journey you looked ready to pass out when you arrived, and Teresa was fussing over you like a hen with one chick. You've been here less than a week, and already you've lost weight and got big-eyed with exhaustion.'

'It's kind of you to be concerned,' she said sarcastically. 'But you're imagining things. I think Mrs Wingard is satisfied with my work.'

'Satisfied! She's worrying about your doing too much. If you work yourself into the ground she'll end up nursing you as well as my father.'

'I'm perfectly fit, thank you. I'm sorry if you were hoping for a big strapping girl, who might have been more to your taste——'

'I thought I'd made it clear that *you* fill that bill quite well,' said Soren. 'Unfortunately.'

So he was back to that again. Lin wrenched her hand from his grasp and stood up. Her voice crisp, she said, 'Yes, isn't it, because you don't do a thing for me!'

She made to step past him, but he said quite pleasantly, 'Let's put that to the test, shall we?' and the next moment he had pulled her against him, with an arm hard about her shoulders, the other hand holding her head while he kissed her ruthlessly. His mouth parted her lips before she had time to resist him, and although she tried to push away, the only effect it had was to make him tighten his hold and deepen the kiss until she felt breathless and dizzy.

When at last he lifted his head to look down at her face, his eyes narrow and glittery, she snapped in a choked voice, 'Let me *go*!' But she sounded bewildered rather than angry, and Soren smiled as though he had some idea of the confusion that raged within her. Because although she was furious with him, the kiss had been far from unpleasant, and she was fighting a shocking desire to lift her mouth again to his and let him kiss her senseless. When he brought his mouth down again to hers, she was terribly afraid that he was going to do it, but her small sound of protest was smothered by his lips. This time he was gentle but extremely thorough, and of its own volition her body seemed to go suddenly pliant and melt against the hard warmth of his, and become a mass of astonished, quivering sensation.

When at last he stopped kissing her, she was glad this time that he was still holding her, because she didn't think she could have stood alone. His lips brushed her temple, and at first she didn't hear the murmured words in her ear, but after a moment the sense of them penetrated. 'Tell me why you came here, Melinda,' he was saying. 'What were you running away from?'

She pushed back from him sharply, and he let her move just enough to stare up into his face. The warmth that had enveloped and dizzied her began to seep away, and she said, 'What do you mean? I'm not running away.' That was true, and the knowledge enabled her to repeat, fiercely, 'I'm *not*!'

Soren looked hard and sceptical, and she struggled suddenly against his arms, until he let her go. Her voice husky with hurt, because he had kissed her to prove a point, and then tried to take advantage of her vulnerability to probe, she asked, 'Why did you say that?'

'Because there's something phoney about you. You're an expensive lady, Melinda——'

'What on *earth* do you mean by that?'

'I'm not blind,' he said curtly. 'Or stupid. Or as trusting as my parents. You came here wearing high-class clothes in a practically brand new car, and toting some very classy luggage. All your working gear is practical, I'll grant you—and it's all brand new. Bought specially for the job.'

'That doesn't prove anything!'

'Absolutely not. It just makes me very curious. Either you're running from something, or you're after something. And I can't think of a thing that a girl like you could be after here, so I figure it's the other.'

So she hadn't been very clever, she surmised. But how was she to know that she would run into someone as sharp and as dangerous as Soren? But he had decided on the wrong alternative, and even as she opened her mouth to give him another denial, she wondered if she should make use of that to throw him off the scent. 'You have a vivid imagination,' she said coldly. 'I'm sure it can come up with some suitably lurid explanation, given time.'

He looked at her consideringly, and drawled, 'I'll give it some thought.'

'I'm sure the results will be fascinating! May I leave now?'

Mockingly, he said, 'What's stopping you? I'll take you back to the house.'

'No, thanks. I'll find my way.'

He leaned over in front of her to open the door, and with his hand on the knob, said, 'Just tell me one thing—is there a man involved?'

She must be careful, but she also wanted to show him she wasn't so easily rattled. She turned to face him, her back against the wall by the door, and said with soft malice, 'Don't tell me you're jealous?'

Soren grinned rather unpleasantly, his eyes glinting. 'No, I won't,' he said, equally softly. 'And don't tell *me* you didn't enjoy that kiss.'

Trying to sound indifferent, she said, 'I'm normal, and your technique isn't too bad.'

'Thank you—I take it you have some experience in these matters.'

'Most girls do, nowadays.'

'True.' His teeth seemed to snap together, and the grin had entirely disappeared. He pulled the door open with a vicious jerk, and waited for her to step out into the sunshine.

'Thank you for showing me the farm,' Lin said as she passed him.

'My pleasure,' he answered with exaggerated politeness, and closed the door behind her as she walked quickly away.

CHAPTER THREE

On Sunday Lin told Teresa she would be out for the day, and she took a picnic lunch and drove to a remote spot at the foot of the Ureweras, where a broad lazy river flowed cold and clear over a rubble of rounded stones. She picked her way through the stones at its edge and dipped her feet in the water, and surveyed the mysterious mountains beyond with their dark, heavy bush covering where the Maori leaders had retreated to lick their wounds after the bitter land wars of the 1860's. Sitting on a grey rock, Lin saw a brilliant blue kingfisher make three abortive dives before coming up triumphant with a silver fish struggling in his cruel beak.

On flat ground in the shade of a puriri sprinkled with pink blossom, she ate her sandwiches and boiled eggs, and wrote a letter to her father. She avoided describing the Wingard family to him, concentrating on the scenery and relaying some of the information that Soren had given her about the farm and its breeding and stock programmes. Her father would be interested in that, if anything. He had been puzzled, perhaps mildly disapproving, when she told him she was going to work for a Mr and Mrs Wingard at Paikea, but the name had not appeared to mean anything to him. He protested a little at the waste of her degree, but she had shrugged and said it was only temporary, just a break in the country.

A little peevishly, he had said, 'Well, I don't know if we can keep your job open for you, my dear.'

'I'll take the risk,' she answered, knowing that her degree

45

was wasted anyway, in the job he had probably created for her if the truth were known, which carried the title of Assistant to the Sales Director but was really a glorified clerkship. She would have preferred to strike out on her own when she left university, but her father had a strongly developed sense of responsibility, and it wasn't his fault that she would rather have had his affection and understanding. She had stopped looking for that some years ago, and yet she had an abnormal fear of hurting or displeasing him, so that she never refused any of the presents he gave her or the things he did for her. Sometimes she told herself in wry self-pity that she was the original poor little rich girl, given everything except the love she longed for. Perhaps her mother had loved her, before she died. Lin remembered her only vaguely, but she did know that Aunt Vera had not been an adequate substitute. It wasn't, she had heard her aunt confide to a friend, as though Lin was *really* one of her family, but of course she would do her best for the poor mite, since Richard had requested her help. It was terribly sad that Marie had died so young, and dreadful for Richard to be left with a child to bring up, especially since she didn't believe that Richard had ever really wanted children in the first place, but had given in to Marie because she pleaded with him to adopt one. Marie had had an idea that a child would bring them closer together, but Richard really wasn't good with children, and quite honestly, Aunt Vera said, she thought he regarded the child as some sort of toy to keep Marie occupied when he was busy. Oh, yes, he was making a very adequate allowance for Melinda's keep, of course. Well, these days, with the best will in the world, one could scarcely afford to keep someone else's child for nothing.

If the allowance her father had paid had been less generous, or he had been less determined to make up to

Lin for all she had been deprived of in the loss of her
mother, her life might paradoxically have been easier. Aunt
Vera, determined to make no profit from her charity,
scrupulously ensured that every cent received was spent on
Lin. Since her own husband had a good job but by no
means the money that Lin's father had, Lin was always
better dressed than her two slightly older cousins, had more
expensive toys and a better furnished bedroom. The natural
outcome of that was the jealousy of her cousins, aggravated
for a time by her own fierce possessiveness, for it wasn't
long before her childish mind conceived that the gifts and
money her father provided were substitutes for love. The
ensuing quarrels between the children must have been hard
for her aunt to bear, and Lin's constant cries of 'You're not
my mummy! I won't!' in the face of the demands of
discipline couldn't have helped much either, she now
realised. Stubborn in her rejection of the truth of her
mother's death, she rejected the new family that she had
been catapulted into, as well. Aunt Vera had done her best,
but Lin had not been a lovable child, only a bewildered,
unhappy and frightened little girl, covering all that terrible
misery with anger and hostility against a world where all
the love and stability she had ever known had disappeared
with terrifying suddenness.

Of course, in time she had settled down and accepted it
all. But it hadn't been easy for any of them, and although
she knew that Aunt Vera and her family grew fond of her,
there was no doubting that when she was sent to boarding
school, the family regarded it as an ideal solution.

She was grateful for those years at boarding school. They
had taught her a lot about self-reliance and self-discipline,
as well as giving her a good academic grounding for her
university studies. She had gone on to the seventh form,
growing into an independent and capable young woman,

moving on to university, and first a hostel, then a shared student flat, without any great trauma, managing to avoid most pitfalls along the way.

Her love affairs had been mild and brief. With a slightly bitter self-knowledge, she knew she was probably more likely than most girls to mistake an infatuation for lasting love, to be too generous in giving her heart to some man to whom she was only a passing fancy. She pitied the girls who had to drop out because they couldn't cope with their personal entanglements and their studies as well, and the girls who came heavily pregnant to class, returning afterwards with haunted eyes because their babies had been given up for adoption, or tired and worried from broken nights nursing a crying infant and rushing in the mornings to deposit the child with some crèche or an obliging relative. It wasn't, she decided, going to happen to her. She gained a reputation for coldness, and didn't care.

Her father had not quite approved of the Australian working holiday after she gained her degree, but Lin had been determined, and his anxiety was easily allayed. He had other things on his mind, a rather tricky merger for one, and anyway, she was over twenty now and there was no point in trying to be heavy-handed. He had given her some good advice, several letters of introduction and some money, told her to write and sent her on her way with his scarcely reluctant blessing.

On her return she had been a little surprised at his insistence that she take a job in his large corporation, and his aggrieved air when at first she had demurred. When he said, 'After all, you're the only child I have,' she had for a few moments wondered fantastically if he meant her to learn the business and follow in his footsteps. But the job, she discovered fairly soon after she started in accordance with his wishes, was a simple dead-end one, and there was no suggestion that she was being trained or groomed for greater things.

He did suggest she move in with him and live in his fashionable town house, and Lin agreed with a leaping of her heart because he really seemed to want her with him. But that was disillusioning, because she seldom saw him without a business colleague or his very efficient secretary of many years' standing. And she soon realised that Miss Oxford envied her with a well-concealed possessiveness towards her boss. Miss Oxford was pathetic rather than malicious, but her determination to keep Richard's attention on herself and the work she alone could help him with increased the distance between Lin and her father. They ate together, and if they were alone he concentrated on paperwork after the evening meal, leaving Lin to her own devices. Living with her father, she was more lonely than ever. It wasn't even as though she could be useful to him, for he saw no reason to change his domestic arrangements beyond letting her cook occasionally at weekends when the woman who cleaned for him didn't come. The solution was obvious —she needed an absorbing occupation. That was when she began the search that had led her eventually to Paikea and in the end to the Wingards. The search that had been first a fleeting thought, an idle longing, then a definite idea, later a challenge to her determination and intelligence and her skill as a researcher, and finally—admittedly—an obsession.

She signed her name to the two-page letter, slipped it into an envelope and wrote her father's name and address on the front. She would write every week and assure him she was well and happy, and that would content him. He would probably write in return occasionally, letters typed by Miss Oxford and just as stilted and uninformative as her own. Communication, of a sort.

She sighed. Like her aunt, he had done his best by her, and it was nobody's fault if his best fell far short of her very real needs. It hadn't been easy for him, either.

Opening the book she had brought along, she tried to read. It proved less interesting than she had hoped, and she found herself drifting into thinking of the one person she had firmly decided to put out of her mind for the day— Soren Wingard.

There was no denying that he was a disturbing factor, one that she hadn't bargained for. Everyone else had accepted her at face value from the start, but Soren had some sort of compulsion to dig beneath the surface.

There was more to it than the sexual tension which he had forced her to admit to herself, if not to him. Her unwilling response to his kiss dismayed and shocked her, because in spite of it she was conscious of a strong personal antagonism for him which contrasted starkly with her immense liking for the other Wingards. And although he had said her signals were muddled, she was convinced that it wasn't only on her side. He was suspicious of her, convinced that she had something to hide, and although it was probably true that she attracted him sexually, he had kissed her mainly in an attempt to throw her off balance and allow him to get through her defences. Soren was a man well able to control his emotions, and there had been no sudden romantic impulse, only a calculated move in a cynical game of his own.

The thought was chilling, and Lin shivered in spite of the warmth of the day, closing her book impatiently. She would move on, explore some of the country roads, and hope that concentrating on her driving and the scenery would banish Soren from her thoughts.

She was back at the farm in time for tea in the evening,

relieved to learn that Soren, too, had been out all day, leaving Tracy and Davy to help their mother with the milking while Susan cooked the meal, and that he was not expected back until late.

'Probably gone to see his girl-friend,' Susan said airily as she turned potatoes in the big roasting dish.

'Does he have one?' asked Lin casually.

'I don't know, really,' Susan admitted. 'Soren's the original clam when it comes to things like that. There's a girl called Rhoda Moers—her father's the manager of the bank in Paikea, I've seen him talking to her a few times, and she's certainly his type, blonde and beautiful. Her people came from Holland, originally.'

Knowing she should leave the subject alone, Lin said lightly, 'How do you know what Soren's "type" is, if he's so—so reticent about his girl-friends?'

'Well, ages ago, he was engaged to a girl called Sonia, and *she* was a stunning blonde, too.'

'What happened?' asked Lin.

'I don't know.' Susan opened the oven door and placed the pan on one of the racks, closed the door and straightened. 'I was too young then to be bothered, except that when he brought her here, I thought it was awfully boring to find them being soppy with each other in corners all the time.'

Lin couldn't help laughing at the picture of the cold, controlled Soren being 'soppy' with anyone, but she found the picture of him in love with the blonde, unknown Sonia and wanting to marry her, curiously disquieting. She wondered if the blighted romance accounted for the dislike of women that she had sensed from their first meeting. Maybe the girl had jilted him and embittered him, a classic situation that gave her no satisfaction, when she thought about it.

'Anyway,' Susan went on, turning to lean against the sink bench with folded arms, 'he hasn't brought a girl home since then, and he's still not married. I think he's quite good-looking, myself,' she added with sisterly judiciousness. 'Do you?'

'I expect he is,' Lin said steadily, 'if you like fair men.'

'Mm, I like them dark and brooding myself. Do you think you could go for Soren, though? Or shouldn't I ask?' Susan grinned, her fair, freckled face colouring a little.

Smiling back to show she had taken no offence, Lin said, 'No, you shouldn't. Soren and I—don't really hit it off.'

'Don't you? Come to think of it, you don't really talk much to each other, do you? There's always so much noise in this family, anyway, I hadn't noticed, but now that you mention it ...' Susan looked thoughtful, then suddenly giggled. 'But that's okay for starters, isn't it? There's some quotation about love being the other side of hate.'

'We don't hate each other,' Lin said hastily. 'We just don't have any—any common ground, that's all.'

It would be too bad if Susan, now of an age to take an inordinate interest in other people's romances, decided to try and pair Lin off with Soren. Changing the subject, she asked, 'Is there anything I can do to help?'

'Heavens, no! It's your day off. Where did you go, anyway?'

Thankfully, Lin took the cue and embarked on a detailed rundown of her day.

The next time she saw Soren wasn't too difficult, because the rest of the family was very much in evidence, their chatter and friendly arguments disguising any signs of discomfort. Not that Soren seemed to feel any. His casual, 'Hello, Melinda,' had the same faintly teasing undertone as always, and she might have imagined the intensified gleam of mockery in his eyes. When she had washed up with help from Davy, whose turn it was, she looked into the sitting room where Soren was talking to his parents, and bade them a general goodnight. It was early, and she would probably watch television in her own room for a while before going to bed. She knew that Teresa and Ray would make her welcome if she wanted to sit with them, but she was anxious not to intrude on their lives. And she might as well be honest, she told herself as she settled in the comfortable chair in her room and watched the credits of a comedy show roll on the screen—she simply didn't want to be around Soren any more than she could help.

It wasn't possible to avoid him altogether, of course, but over the next few weeks, while she settled down to a work routine that was less frenetic than her first few days, and into a remarkably happy and comfortable relationship with the other members of the family, she did manage to treat Soren with polite indifference that was just short of unfriendliness, and to ensure that they were never alone together.

For his part, Soren didn't seek her out and seemed to accept that she had no desire to talk to him apart from the demands of common courtesy. But he watched her. With the family chatter going on around them, Lin would feel the weight of his gaze on her, and look up to find his eyes resting on her face, speculative and watchful. He didn't bother to look away when she raised her own eyes in a silent challenge. In fact, she thought that it amused him.

One day when Teresa had been into Paikea during the afternoon, she amused them all at the table that evening with a humorous description of a misunderstanding that had occurred in the post office, between herself and the girl at the counter. 'Honestly, that poor girl,' she finished. 'She simply doesn't have a clue! If the postmaster wasn't her father, she wouldn't have lasted five minutes in that job.'

Soren said, 'She shouldn't have been given it in the first place. She's a menace.'

'Well, she's rather dim, I admit,' his stepmother agreed. 'But she does her best. She's a nice girl.'

'Is that supposed to make up for her complete incompetence at her job?' Soren demanded, but he smiled at Teresa even as he said it. 'Surely it would have been better all round if her father had found her a job she could cope with adequately.'

'That's easier said than done, and she might have got into all sorts of trouble if she had to go away from him, you know. She's quite pretty, too.'

'Yes, and trades on it to try and cover up her shortcomings in other directions,' Soren said icily. 'And I don't see that she's any more likely to get into trouble than any of the other girls who've had to go away to work. She isn't actually retarded, surely?'

'Heavens, no! But you can't blame her parents for wanting to keep her under their wing.'

'I do, when the rest of us have to suffer for it,' Soren retorted. 'I had to take one of their accounts back three times, trying to sort out the muddle she'd made of it, and in the end her father had to be called in to straighten things out.'

Lin glanced up quickly. And briefly, as though her eyes had drawn his, he met her gaze. He gave the ghost of a smile and a nod, confirming her guess that the last occasion had been the day she had arrived in Paikea. Neither of them had mentioned their brief encounter in the post office that day, and for the first time it occurred to her that it was odd that no one in the family knew they had met before being introduced after she arrived at the house.

Susan and Tracy had been taking little notice of the discussion, having a murmured debate of their own while it
went on. Now, as the conversation lapsed, Susan looked up
and said, 'There's a dance on next Saturday night. Can we
go?' She looked appealingly at her mother and then her
father, and Lin had the impression that her hands were
tightly clasped together under the table.

Ray and Teresa looked questioningly at each other, and
Tracy, her blue eyes shining softly, said, 'A lot of the kids
from school are going. Carol Anson's mother is letting *her*
go.'

'Is it a teenage dance?' Ray asked them.

'No.' Susan looked uncertain whether this was likely to
make her parents look more favourably on the idea. 'Older
people can go, too.' She cast a quick glance under golden-
brown lashes at Soren, and added, 'Rhoda Moers said she'd
be there.'

Lin saw Soren give his half-sister a rather penetrating
glance, but he said nothing.

Ray said, 'You can't go on your own, you two,' and
Tracy said eagerly, 'What if Lin came with us? We thought
maybe she'd like to——'

Lin caught the look of appeal that went with that, and
said swiftly, 'I'm sure I would. We can go in my car, and I
promise to look after the girls, Ray.'

Ray looked over at his wife, his face still doubtful, and
Soren said, 'I'll take you.'

Teresa and Ray relaxed, and Susan squealed, '*Will* you,
Soren? What a super big brother you are!' She gave him
a saucy smile, and he returned it with a glint in his eyes.
Susan pursed her lips in mock demureness, peeping at him
from under her lashes, and Soren laughed, leaned across
the table and tweaked at her hair.

Watching them, Lin thought how different Soren looked

when he laughed like that, banishing every hint of austerity, his eyes warm and teasing. He turned his head a little and met her gaze, the warmth still in his eyes. The laughter faded from his face, and he looked slightly questioning. For a moment she was held by that questioning glance, then Tracy pulled at his sleeve to gain his attention, and he turned away.

Lin dressed with care for the dance, in a pretty silk-look synthetic dress with narrow shoulder straps, a figure-hugging bodice and a swirling full skirt. The material was patterned in shades of blue from peacock to powder blue, and she used a blue eyeshadow to enhance the colour of her eyes. She brushed mascara over the tips of her lashes, coloured her mouth pink with a lip gloss, and left her shining hair free, swinging softly against her shoulders, except for two strands drawn from her temples to the back of her head, and secured with a tortoiseshell comb.

She was slipping on her black, high-heeled sandals when Susan knocked on her door and peeped in.

'Come in,' said Lin. 'I'm ready.' She opened her wardrobe to pull out a triangular black silk shawl and toss it about her shoulders.

'Hey, you look stunning!' Susan exclaimed admiringly.

'Thank you. You look super, yourself.'

'Soren says I look like a daffodil,' Susan giggled. 'I'm not sure if it's a compliment or not,' she added, looking down at her pretty yellow dress: 'He's here, by the way. He said he's ready when we are.'

When they came into the sitting room Tracy, flushed and youthfully lovely in white broderie anglaise, bounced to her feet as though she couldn't wait another minute. Soren, sitting on the sofa talking to his father, turned his head and rose more slowly, his eyes on Lin. She saw the flicker of something in his eyes, and knew with a faint sense of triumph that her appearance had affected him. Soren himself looked elegantly casual in dark pants and a shirt that was made of some silky knit, the sleeves fuller than usual, giving it a dressy look, and the collar open to show a beaten silver medallion resting on his tanned chest.

Ray and Teresa admired all three of the girls and told them to have a good time. As they went out to Soren's car, and he opened the front passenger door for Lin while his half-sisters took the back seat, Lin felt his sidelong gaze on her. When he came round to his own seat and started the engine, Susan leaned on the seat back behind him and said, 'Hey—if I'm a daffodil, what's Tracy?'

Soren grinned and cast a quick glance over his shoulder. 'A daisy?' he suggested lazily.

Susan said, 'What about Lin, then?'

Lin stared straight ahead as the car nosed out of the gateway and headed for the road. Soren took his time, but she knew he had passed a swift glance over her. Then he said slowly, 'An orchid, of course.'

'Oh, yes!' Susan said delightedly. 'She does look exotic and—and sort of fragile in that dress, doesn't she? Don't you think it's gorgeous?'

'I do.'

Lin said, 'I'm not at all fragile or exotic, actually.'

Soren laughed a little. 'Orchids in their native state are a jungle flower, tough and determined to survive.'

'Lin isn't tough,' Susan said positively. 'She's nice.'

'Thank you, Susan,' Lin said lightly. She cast a quick, quizzical look at Soren, and caught the slight down-turned smile he gave her in acknowledgement. They understood each other perfectly. *Nice* was not a word he would have used of her. She wondered if she might ask him, later, how he would describe her, and felt a small stirring of something like excitement. Soren challenged her, and she had never shirked a challenge. She could stand up to him.

When they arrived at the hall, the girls swept Lin off to meet their friends, and she soon found herself dancing with a clumsy though well-meaning youth who must have been all of eighteen years old. She saw Soren dancing with a tall, strikingly blonde girl who had a beautiful figure played up by a slinky slim dress of bright red that few women could have worn successfully. But she did—superbly, Lin admitted. Rhoda Moers, undoubtedly. There couldn't be two girls answering so accurately to Susan's description in a place the size of Paikea.

They made a handsome couple, and not a few eyes were following the two of them, with varying degrees of interest and envy.

When the dance was over, and her partner returned Lin to her seat between Susan and Tracy, she saw Soren coming towards them with Rhoda on his arm. Susan saw them too, and jumped up, saying, 'Hello, Rhoda, I told Soren you'd be here.'

Rhoda's fair complexion couldn't hide the faint blush that rose to her cheeks, and Susan looked abashed as Soren directed a quelling look at her. He pulled Susan's vacated chair out a little for Rhoda, and introduced her to Lin, as Susan hovered at her brother's elbow.

Rhoda's smile was friendly and rather dazzling. 'Soren's been telling me about you,' she said. 'You come from Auckland?'

'Yes.' Lin shot a glance up at Soren, whose face was quite expressionless.

'What on earth made you come to a little one-horse place like Paikea?' Rhoda asked, laughing.

Warily, Lin said, 'I like the country, and the job sounded interesting. I'm enjoying it.'

Rhoda made a wry face. 'Housework? Heavens! I must say, you don't look the domesticated type.'

Mildly, Lin said, 'I don't know what "the domesticated type" should look like, do you?'

Rhoda looked rueful. 'Did I put my foot in it?' she asked frankly. 'I didn't mean anything disparaging.'

'No, of course you didn't,' Lin assured her quickly. 'I take it you're not keen on housework.'

'Mm-mm.' Rhoda emphatically shook her head. 'What were you doing before?'

'I had an office job,' Lin answered with some reserve. 'It was very boring. What do *you* do?'

'At the moment I'm working in a dress shop in the town, but as soon as I can, I'm getting out. I had a job in Auckland, but a few months ago I came down with hepatitis—a nasty bug, that. It takes a long time to get over it, so I came home to recuperate. What I really want to do is travel. Have you ever been overseas, Lin?'

Lin hesitated. This girl bothered her. She seemed friendly and open and her questions might have been idle curiosity or simply showing a flattering interest in a new acquaintance. But Soren, apparently gazing about the room and taking no part in their conversation, was quite close enough to hear it. She couldn't help wondering if he had asked his girl-friend to try and find out more about Lin than she had told him.

'I had a working holiday in Australia,' she said cautiously.

'Sounds like fun. Where did you go?'

Lin told her, and the other girl listened, apparently rapt. 'Whereabouts in Auckland do you come from?' she asked, rather suddenly.

After the briefest of pauses Lin said, 'I was flatting with some other girls in Epsom for a while.'

'Oh, we had a place in Parnell,' said Rhoda. 'I love Auckland.'

The band had begun to play again, and Rhoda stretched out a hand to Soren, smiling up at him. 'Are you going to dance with me again?' she asked him gaily. 'I love that tune!'

He pulled her up into his arms, and they moved away, Rhoda's fair head tilted to an enchanting angle as she spoke to Soren, who looked down at her with a faint, sometimes amused smile.

Lin danced with another young man, less clumsy and more articulate than her previous partner. The two Wingard girls were enjoying themselves with the young crowd, but Lin, between dances, felt a little out of place. The talk seemed to be mainly of school, the imminent examinations, and the whereabouts and romantic entanglements of people she didn't know. She was relieved when Soren came and asked her to dance, and he noted her prompt acceptance with slight surprise in his smile. 'Enjoying yourself?' he asked.

'Yes.'

'But not wildly, it seems.'

'Everyone's very nice,' she said. 'It's just that the girls and their crowd are much younger than I am, that's all.'

'Poor Grandma!' he mocked. 'You don't look much older than they are, you know.'

'Well, it so happens that I'm not a schoolgirl,' she said tartly.

There was a glint in the eyes that swept over her appraisingly. 'No, you're not, are you?' Soren said softly, and his arm pulled her perceptibly closer as they danced.

'That wasn't an invitation,' Lin said hardily.

He laughed softly. 'I know. Just a gentle reminder. As if I needed it.'

She made a move to widen the distance between them, but he wouldn't let her, his hand hard on her waist, and his fingers tightening just a little on hers. Lin stiffened for a few moments, but then relaxed. He was a very good dancer, and the music and the movement of their bodies in unison almost mesmerised her.

When the music stopped Soren said, 'You're good. Come and meet some other people.'

At one end of the hall a few tables had been set out on a carpeted area, and he seated her at one of these with Rhoda and a young engaged couple. He introduced her to several other people, and stayed by her side until the music began again, and someone else swept Rhoda on to the floor. Then he turned to her with his hand held out, and she got up and followed him on to the floor.

The next dance was claimed by one of the men she had just met, and then Soren surprised her by asking her again, and then a fourth time. As he steered her on to the floor, she looked back at Rhoda still sitting at the table, her finger idly tracing a pattern on its top. 'Why did you ask me?' she asked Soren as his arms closed about her. 'Not Rhoda?'

His eyes were enigmatic. 'I wanted to ask you,' he said. 'Not Rhoda.'

'You know what I mean.'

'Do I? Did you think she might be jealous?'

'I thought she might be—hurt.'

Rather harshly, he said, 'She doesn't have the right.'

Lin glanced at him fleetingly. There was something un-pleasantly grim about the set of his mouth, and she won-dered if Rhoda had annoyed him by appearing too possessive.

'She said, 'Rhoda's a nice girl.'

'Very nice,' he agreed, sounding bored.

With a spurt of temper, Lin said, 'I won't let you use me

to—teach her a lesson, if that's what you're doing.'

'Oh, for God's sake!' he snapped. 'Shut up!'

'What?' Lin stopped dancing to stare indignantly into his face.

Between clenched teeth, Soren muttered, 'Come here——'

She felt his fingers digging into her arm as he almost dragged her through a side door into the darkness outside. She nearly stumbled as he pulled her around a corner of the building, and the next moment he had pushed her against the wall and turned her face up with his hands to meet his fierce kiss.

His body pressed against hers, and when she raised her hands in a feeble effort to ward him off, he fought them down easily and held them at her sides as he went on kissing her until she was breathless and dizzy. His mouth was warm and possessive and inescapable. And with dismay she realised that she didn't want him to stop. When he did stop, moving a little away, but with his hands now clamped against the wall on either side of her face, she was glad of its support behind her.

'So now will you shut up?' he said in a soft snarl. 'Rhoda has nothing to do with this. This is between you and me, Melinda, so leave her out of it.'

Before she could recover her breath, he had grasped her arm again and was propelling her back into the hall. The music had changed to a slow, dreamy number, and as soon as they regained the floor, Soren jerked her into his arms almost roughly, and held her close as they moved about the floor in time to the music. The lights had been dimmed, adding to the intimacy of this style of dancing. Vaguely she saw the pale gleam of Rhoda's hair as she drifted by with another man, and Susan's yellow skirt flaring out as her partner tried a tricky turn. Soren's breath stirred her hair as he muttered, 'Relax, Melinda. I can't make violent love to you here.'

She quivered, and made bold by the dimness, murmured, 'Do you want to?'

She felt his body tauten and the faint tremor that matched her own. His voice flat and stark, he said, 'Yes.'

CHAPTER FOUR

LIN danced with no one else that evening. Other people spoke to her and she must have talked to them, but afterwards she could recall no conversation. She was conscious only of Soren, of his arms about her when they danced, of his presence beside her when they were not dancing. They didn't speak to each other and didn't touch except when they danced. They scarcely even looked at each other, and yet the awareness was so strong Lin knew every tiny movement that he made—as she knew very well that he was conscious of hers. She was vaguely aware that Rhoda was dancing lightheartedly with several successive partners, but that her smile occasionally slipped when she was not dancing. She saw Tracy looking at herself and Soren dancing, and looking again with surprise and puzzlement. She remembered to make sure that Susan and Tracy were in sight and enjoying themselves. But all the time the strange, dark flame within her burned more strongly, and its centre was Soren. All the other people in the crowded hall were shadows dancing at the edge of this sudden, inexplicable fire.

Soren drove them home fast and in silence, while the two girls whispered and laughed in the back, and Lin sat beside him with her eyes fixed on the road swept by their headlights, her bare arm brushing the silky sleeve of his shirt.

When he drew up outside the house, he got out and opened the back door first on the driver's side. Susan and Tracy slid out, and he waited for them. Tracy stood on tiptoe to kiss his cheek and say, 'Thank you, Soren.' And

Susan murmured something that made him grin and give her behind a smart slap as she passed him.

The tension broke, and Lin, suddenly afraid of being left alone with him, fumbled open the catch of the car door and got out, snapping it shut behind her as she came around the hood and made to pass Soren, and follow the two girls up the short path to the house.

As she reached him, Soren's hand came out swiftly and locked on her arm. Her breath seemed to stop in her throat. His eyes in the moonlight looked fathoms deep, and she couldn't see the expression on his face.

Susan turned in the doorway and said, 'Lin——?' And Tracy shushed her and pulled her inside. Her surprised, muffled protest brought a faint grin to Soren's face, and as Lin moved her arm he dropped his hand to his side. 'I'll see you tomorrow,' he said.

Of course he would, but he meant, *be with me tomorrow.* So she said, 'Yes.'

His hand lifted again and lightly touched her cheek. Then he was on his way back to the car, and Lin turned and fled up the path to the house.

The next morning when she came out for breakfast, Susan looked at her with expectant curiosity, then suddenly jumped slightly and lowered her head over her cornflakes with diligence that made Lin suspect that Tracy had kicked her older sister under cover of the table. In some ways the quieter Tracy was more mature than her ebullient sister, and Lin was grateful for her tact. She didn't want to be plied with questions about Soren or about last night.

In the clear light of morning, what had happened last night seemed incredible. Soren had kissed her, had danced with her and held her close, and she had responded like a mind-less doll with no will of her own. And she had promised—

what had she promised, with that fatal 'yes'? What would he expect of her if she spent today with him?

She must have been mad last night—moon-madness, that's what it was. And Soren—had he been a little mad, too, or had he merely manipulated her, deliberately and in cold blood?

That was a horrible thought, but it could be true. Soren was curious about her, and didn't quite trust her motives. He still looked at her at times with that coldly speculating light in his eyes. He was basically a scientist, and he had decided she was an interesting specimen of womanhood. She sometimes felt that he was mentally putting her under a microscope for dissection. Like the time he had come in and found her coaching Susan in history. She hadn't wanted to carry on with Soren there, but she couldn't just abruptly stop, and Susan was listening eagerly to her knowledgeable backgrounding on the colonial expansion of the nineteenth century.

Soren listened too, leaning against the bench with his hands in his pockets and watching her with evident interest. When Susan had gone, he asked her, 'You have a degree in history?'

She hadn't wanted the Wingards to know, but a direct lie would make too much of it. 'How did you guess?' she asked lightly, and he said,

'That wasn't High School stuff you were spouting just now, or general knowledge. You know your subject.'

'Thank you.'

'A bit wasted here, isn't it?' he commented.

'Not at all. Susan found it very useful, I think.'

'Are you a teacher?'

'No.' Lin pulled a bowl of potatoes along the bench to the sink. Soren moved a little to give her room, but not enough.

'How long since you left university?' he asked her.

She didn't see what he could make of that, so she said, 'A year, almost.' She was running water into the sink, slipping off her watch to deposit it on the windowsill.

But he made something of it, all right. His eyes glinting with curiosity, Soren commented, 'You've done well for yourself in that time. A snazzy car, pricey clothes—this——' He picked up her watch and examined the fine gold expanding bracelet and the tiny diamonds round the face. 'Very nice,' he commented.

Lin began peeling a potato as he replaced the watch on the sill.

'It was a gift,' she said shortly.

'And the car?'

'That, too!' she snapped. She shouldn't have let him rattle her into saying that. She should have said it was on hire-purchase—or, better still, said nothing at all. It was nothing to do with him.

Teresa had come in just then, and she was spared the dilemma of deciding whether to tell him that her father had given her both car and watch. She didn't want to talk about her father or mother to the Wingards. Teresa knew that Lin's mother had died when she was a child, that she had been brought up by her aunt, and that her father had an office in Auckland, but Lin had been purposely reticent about her family. She had told no lies, but she had not been forthcoming, either. She didn't want them connecting her with the Blake business enterprises. When she dropped out of their lives, she didn't want them to be able to find her. She had been careful from the start, using a box number as her address on the letter she had sent asking about the job, giving only her telephone number away.

But she had known that Soren hadn't given up. His mind was the kind that didn't give up. It would keep digging at a problem until he had solved it. And he saw her as a problem—as in maths.

She strongly suspected that Rhoda's questioning had been on his behalf, last night. The girl hadn't really shown much personal interest in the answers, but Soren, she was sure, had been listening intently. Was Rhoda his girl? He had denied it—or had he? She had no rights over him, he had said. Lin doubted he would allow any woman rights, he reserved those to himself. And then he had said, *Leave her out of it* and *Rhoda has nothing to do with this*. It wasn't exactly a denial of involvement with her.

All through breakfast she was rehearsing and discarding little speeches refusing to go anywhere with Soren today. But he must have mentioned it to Ray and Teresa, because they seemed to be taking it for granted, when they came in. Ray had been helping again with the milking lately, and limping about the farm without a stick. 'Take the day off,' he said when Soren strolled in and said to Lin, 'Ready?' and to Ray, 'I'll be home in time for milking.'

'We'll cope,' said Ray, and Soren exchanged a lightning glance with Teresa, who nodded imperceptibly.

Lin sat in Soren's car wondering what he expected of this day, of *her*. She was almost suffocatingly aware of him beside her as he turned on to the road and made for the coast. He didn't talk, and she couldn't think of anything to say. Last night had taken them beyond small talk, and anything else was—dangerous.

Eventually the road took them near the sea, long stretches of breakers rolling on to white sand strung with weekend fishermen casting into the surf, and far away in the distance an island volcano lazily puffing white smoke into a cloud-spattered sky. On the horizon the blue of the sea and the sky merged into each other, and when the road climbed a little and they were looking down on the water as it kissed the shore, the intensity of its clear azure colour was breath-taking. Native plants clung to the white cliffs that plunged down to the sea's edge, ending abruptly in slivers of pale sand along the shore.

They stopped for a snack at a popular beach, and afterwards Lin asked for the first time, 'Are we going anywhere in particular?'

'Some place private,' said Soren, glancing at the family parties and strolling young couples surrounding them.

'It's—quite nice here,' she said.

'It's even nicer further on,' he told her, and opened the door of the car.

Some time later, as the car climbed a steep, winding road, where the sea washed lazily blue at the foot of the cliff, he pulled up on a grass verge, and turned his head to look at her.

Lin kept her troubled gaze on the surging sea below and the curvetting of the gulls that skimmed its surface and then flung themselves screaming into the air.

Soren put out his hand, brushed a strand of hair back from her face and touched her cheek with his knuckles. 'What's the matter?' he asked.

'Nothing. Can we get out for a while?'

He lowered his hand and said, 'Yes, if you like.' But Lin hadn't waited for his reply, and was already opening her door.

'Be careful,' he said, as she walked to the cliff edge and looked over at the tumbled vegetation that covered it to the strip of white sand below. She stepped back as he joined her. 'There's a path,' she said. 'It must go down to the beach.'

It was narrow and steep, but there was a wooden hand-rail and it was well used.

Soren went down it a little way, peered over the railing,

and looked back at her. 'It looks okay,' he said. 'Coming?'

Lin hesitated, then shook her head. 'No, I don't think so.'

He came back to her and asked quietly, 'Are you afraid of heights?'

She shook her head again, looking nervously away from him.

'Then you're afraid of me.'

'Of course not!' She looked up angrily and caught his sceptical gaze on her face.

'There's no need,' he said rather gently, and took her hand. 'Come on.'

She followed him down the winding path, where pungas, manuka and taller trees jostled each other for room on the steep slope. At the bottom the sand was soft and cool in the shade of the trees, warmer where the sun caught it at the water's edge. Lin slipped off her sandals and let the wave-lets trickle over her bare feet, while Soren watched her, leaning against a tree with his arms folded.

When she turned and came slowly back to where he stood, he straightened as she approached, his eyes unread-able. She stopped a few feet away, then suddenly veered a little and sat down on the sand, trying to brush the clinging stuff from her feet so that she could replace her sandals.

Soren said, 'You'd better let them dry.'

'Yes,' she said, and sat still, her head a little bent, so that a gentle breeze lifted the hair at her nape. She didn't realise that Soren had moved and dropped to the sand behind her, until his fingers pushed aside the remaining strands, and she felt his lips warmly caress her skin.

'Don't——' she said huskily. 'Please don't!'

His hand grasped her shoulder, turning her in his arms until he could tip her face with a hand under her chin. 'You knew when you said yes last night that I wanted to make love to you.'

She couldn't deny that, he had certainly told her that was what he wanted. Her eyes dropped from his, and she began to struggle. Soren held her a few moments longer, his mouth curving in grim amusement at her futile efforts to free herself. Then he let her go suddenly and said, 'Playing hard to get, Melinda?'

Her shoulders hunched as she turned away from him, she said, 'No! I'm—sorry, if I gave you the wrong impression last night. I don't want you to make love to me, Soren.'

'In the cold light of day?'

'I suppose so. The moonlight and the music must have got to me.' She tried to speak lightly, turning to him with a brief little half smile, but the smile he gave her in return was less than pleasant, and there was an angry glitter in his eyes. She looked away again rather quickly, and said jerkily, 'Shall we go?'

Lin scrambled to her feet quickly in case he came to help her, but he got to his feet in his own good time, letting her lead the way back up the cliff.

She climbed so quickly that she was panting when she reached the top. She leaned against the car, getting back her breath, and trying to wipe the sand from her feet on the springy grass. Soren pulled a clean handkerchief from his pocket, shook out the folds and gave it to her. She said, 'Thank you,' on a note of some surprise. His anger had faded, she saw, and he seemed amused as he watched her rubbing at the sand and struggling into her sandals. As she swung her legs into the car, he took the handkerchief from her fingers and pushed it back into his pocket. When he got into his seat beside her, he didn't immediately start the car, but rested his arm on the steering wheel, half turning to face her.

'Do you want to have dinner in Whakatane, or go straight home?' he asked her.

'That's up to you.'

'Then we'll have dinner first.' He paused. 'And maybe get to know each other a little better.'

Lin cast him a swift, wary glance.

'That's what bothers you, isn't it?' he asked her. 'You suddenly found yourself in at the deep end, no preliminary paddling in the shallows. And you're out of your depth.'

He was right, but that was only a part of it. Cautiously she said, 'I'm not sure I know what you're talking about.'

His voice hardening a little, he retorted, 'Yes, you do. You may not like me much, but you *know* there's something between us that's a hell of a lot stronger than liking.'

She couldn't deny that. There was sexual awareness between them, so strong that she knew every time Soren came into a room, even if she had her back to the door. It had led her into betraying herself last night, and she wasn't sure yet that he had not been using it to take her off her guard and satisfy his curiosity. But mixed with it was a welter of other emotions, anger and resentment—she resented him, she admitted it—and distrust. She had even been sure at times that Soren positively disliked her.

'It isn't love,' she said finally.

'I know that.' His voice was quiet.

'It's not enough,' she said.

'For what?'

'For—a love affair. For—anything.'

'Surely it's enough to make us want to explore further? To find out what else we have in common, to get to know each other better?'

If he was sincere, that would be a terrible temptation. But even if he meant it, if he wasn't just trying to pry information from her, she dared not embark on any discovery with Soren. The complications could be horrendous. She said, trying to hide the sudden hollow feeling inside her, 'The start of a beautiful friendship?' He didn't smile, and she said, 'No. I don't want to start—anything.'

'It's already started. Do you think you can call a halt, just like that?'

'That's what I'm doing.' She was pleased that her voice sounded crisp and decisive, which wasn't at all the way she felt.

'You can't just turn your back on it and pretend it isn't there,' he said. 'I won't let you.'

Lin looked down at her clenched hands and said fiercely, 'I don't *want* it, Soren. Please leave me alone.'

There was a long silence, then he said, 'No.'

Lin trembled. 'You don't understand,' she said despairingly.

'No, I don't. Make me understand, then.'

'I—can't.'

'You won't even try?'

Mutely she shook her head. She couldn't confide in him. Heaven knew what damage it would do.

She looked up at him, her eyes pleading. 'Please leave it, Soren.'

He gave a small nod, his mouth grim, and turned away from her to switch on the engine.

They had reached Whakatane before she asked, 'Have you almost finished your report?'

He glanced at her. 'Almost.'

'And are you going to take that leave you were talking of?'

'I don't know yet. My father seems pretty fit, but he shouldn't try to do too much yet. Were you hoping I'd leave soon?'

'Of course not.' But she had been wondering how much longer he would stay.

She relapsed into silence as he drove along the shoreline

and stopped the car at a headland, where a bronze statue of a woman stood, her body proudly naked, and her hair apparently streaming in the wind.

'Who is she?' she asked him.

'That's Wairaka, a sort of early Maori Women's Libber. When the great migration of the Maori occurred, the canoe commanded by her father, or husband, I'm not sure which, landed here, and the men all leapt ashore to explore, leaving their women and children behind. The canoe began to drift out to sea, and the women were helpless because paddling was men's work and there was a sort of sacredness about it. None of them dared touch a paddle—except Wairaka, who picked one up eventually and brought the canoe to the shore, saying something like, "I must be a man," or "I will take a man's role." The Maori phrase starts with the word *Whakatane* anyway, and that's how the place got it's name.'

Lin said slowly, 'She doesn't sound like a Women's Libber to me. Lots of women deserted by their men have to make decisions and take action to save their children—in all sorts of ways.'

'You mean she acted from necessity, not choice?'

'Yes.'

'But all the other women just wept and wailed. Wairaka acted.'

'Oh, yes. She was a leader. But I expect she wasn't allowed to do much leading when the men were about.'

'Times are changing,' said Soren. 'And a good thing too.'

She looked at him curiously. 'You believe it is? Equal rights?'

'Yes, of course. Don't you? I'd have picked you for a feminist.'

'I am!' she said emphatically. 'But I would never have picked you for an advocate of women's rights.'

'Which shows you have a lot to learn about me.'

She learned more about him over their leisurely dinner. Afterwards she couldn't have said what they ate, only that it was delicious. Soren was entertaining and humorous and informative, and she enjoyed hearing him talk. When he questioned her about her life, and her experiences, she was cautious, and answered briefly for the most part, careful to give little away. And he would watch her with a slight, wry smile, and gracefully accept the conversational ball when she passed it back to him. She learned that he had a degree in Agricultural Science and a couple of diplomas in aspects of milk processing. She discovered that he liked the same kind of music as she did, and some of the same books. For a while, because these were fairly safe subjects, she became relaxed enough to argue with him amicably on the merits of certain literary and musical works and concur with his opinions of others.

As they drove home afterwards the stars were pricking the sky in pinpoints of light, and as the darkness deepened and a huge orange moon hung over the hills, the scattering of stars became a lavish, multitudinous display of breath-taking brilliance. The Milky Way spilled across the heavens in a pale blur studded with tiny bright spangles, and the Southern Cross hung against its velvety black background as though it was newly minted.

Moonlight shimmered over the landscape, rippled over the sea when they glimpsed it, and glowed through the leaves of the trees at the roadside. The night was so beautiful that it was almost intoxicating, and when Lin leaned forward in her seat to view the stars better, her mouth parting in a soft sound of admiration, she saw Soren turn his head briefly and smile as though he understood.

When at last they were home, it wasn't really late, and lights still gleamed from the windows of the house. Soren got out of the car and opened the door for Lin while she was still bemusedly fiddling with the catch. When she stood beside him, she couldn't help raising her face to the sky, reluctant to go inside the house and shut out the glorious night.

The moon was high and silvery white, now, its cool lustre reflected by Soren's fair hair when she turned to face him. The shadows softened the angles and planes of his face.

She said, 'Thank you for today, Soren.'

'You enjoyed yourself?'

'Yes. And it's such a beautiful night.'

'I can't take credit for that. But the moon deserves her tribute, don't you think?'

He took her shoulders firmly and pulled her close, his mouth gentle and coaxing as he kissed her slowly and with great deliberation. Lin knew her lips were parting, knew that she should curb her response, but when Soren moved one hand to her waist to draw her closer, her body simply curved meltingly into his, and her hands went up to his shoulders and linked behind his neck. His mouth had the same deep, dark hypnotic quality as the warm night that lapped about them, and she didn't try to stop him.

When he drew away, still lightly holding her waist with his hands, she said, 'A tribute to the moon?'

'That's right. And to you, for being beautiful, like the night.' His hand touched her hair softly, stroking it back from her face, shaping her ear with a gentle finger. 'You're lovely,' he said. 'A moon goddess.'

If anyone else had said that to her she would probably have laughed at his extravagance. She wasn't a goddess, but Soren had magic in his fingertips, and she suddenly felt like one.

'I always knew there was something of the pagan about

you,' she said. 'You're a Viking, strong and fierce and——'

'Predatory?' he said, with a brief, soft laugh.

He was still holding her, and her hands lay against his chest, the warmth of his body under the thin shirt coming through to her palms. Quite seriously she said, 'You're not a predator, are you?'

And he said quietly, 'No, I'm not.'

Lin moved a little, then, and Soren dropped his hands from her and let her step back. She asked, 'Are you coming in?'

'Yes. The folks seem to be still up. We might be in time for a cup of coffee.'

He took her hand and held it, and they went into the house like that, then on to the sitting room where the rest of the family was watching television, and as they entered they were still holding hands.

CHAPTER FIVE

LIN woke the next morning with a delicious feeling of well-being, thrusting to the back of her mind the dismayed thought that she should never have allowed what had happened last night. She had a reckless desire to live each day as it came, and never count tomorrow.

Soren had a late breakfast with Ray and Teresa, and came back later for lunch, but there was no chance for any private talk with him. And Lin was suddenly attacked by shyness, after she smiled her good morning to him, and saw the way he looked at her, with startling intimacy, as he drawled, 'Good morning, Melinda.'

In the afternoon Ray went off to help with the milking, and Lin had Scott to look after as well as a meal to prepare. She gave him some fat crayons and blank newsprint paper while she began to peel vegetables, and he chattered to her happily as he drew incomprehensible pictures in vivid colours, every now and then demanding her admiration. Lin gave it absentmindedly, her thoughts not on her task but on the events of last night.

Rinsing the peeled potatoes and carrots, she suddenly realised that she had neglected to take some meat from the big freezer in the laundry off the back porch. Chiding herself for not keeping her mind on her work, she rushed out to remedy her omission, sorting through frozen packs until her fingers were numb. Finally she found some lamb chops and took them back into the kitchen. Scott was not there, and she called his name as she tipped the chops into a roasting dish and dusted them with salt and pepper.

He didn't answer, and after pushing the dish into the oven, Lin went out into the passage, and then down to his room, but there was no sign of the child. He wasn't in the bathroom, either, and she began to worry as she went out the back door and looked about.

She saw Soren's tall figure first, striding towards the house from the milking shed, and then she saw the small figure running over the grass to meet him. Soren swung the child into his arms, and met her at the gateway in the fence that surrounded the house. Scott must have climbed it to get out.

'What was he doing out there?' Soren demanded as she swung the gate wide to let them in.

His eyes held no warmth for her, and his tone was peremptory. Defensively, Lin said, 'He must have run out while I was getting some meat for tea. It wasn't more than five minutes, but——'

'Five minutes is more than enough for this tyke,' Soren snapped. He swung Scott down, went down on his haunches in front of him, and said sternly. 'When Lin's looking after you, stay put! You're not to run away from her, understand?'

Guileless blue eyes stared into his hard green ones. Scott put a thumb to his mouth and nodded silently.

'Right, now go along inside, and behave yourself.' Soren turned him in the direction of the door and gave him a smart slap on his small rump to emphasise the point. Scott cast him a reproachful glare and trotted obediently up the steps and through the door.

Feeling it was probably her turn for chastisement, Lin said, 'I'm sorry. He seemed so absorbed in his play, I didn't think he'd even notice I wasn't there for a few minutes.'

'He'd notice all right. As sharp as a new pin, is our Scott

—and as fast as a greased pig. He needs watching every second.'

'I'll remember,' Lin said stiffly. 'It won't happen again.'

'I wouldn't bet on it,' Soren said grimly.

Lin flared. 'I *said* it won't happen again! It *won't*!'

She turned and hurried up the steps, but as she reached the doorway, Soren caught up with her and then gripped her arm. 'Hold on——' he ordered.

'*Don't touch me!*' She pulled away, but his grip tightened, and he took her other arm as well, turning her to face him.

'That isn't what you said last night,' he said, with laughter in his voice.

Lin's head came up and she glared at him. He laughed outright then, saying, 'Good lord, you look exactly like Scott! Maybe I should administer the same treatment.'

Colouring furiously, she snapped, 'Don't you damn well *dare*!'

'Don't dare me, Melinda,' he warned softly. 'Listen——'

Struggling, she said, 'Let me *go*! I have work to do, Mr Wingard. As you just reminded me, I'm supposed to be watching Scott——'

'Lin——'

'So just let me get on with it, will you?'

'*For God's sake, shut up, will you?*' he muttered between clenched teeth, and suddenly jerked her fully into his arms and found her mouth with a punishing kiss, brief and bruising.

When he lifted his head she was speechless with shock, and he said, '*Now* will you listen to me?' He loosened his hold and let her slip out of it. 'I wasn't criticising you when I said I wouldn't bet on Scott not getting away from you again. I know from experience he's a determined little Houdini, and I wouldn't blame you if he managed to outwit you again. I trust you not to let him get too far, but you need warning that he's not easy to keep an eye on.'

'You certainly blamed me for it today,' she said.

'If it sounded like it, I'm sorry. I got a bit of a fright when I saw him so far from home, and you weren't in sight. I'm fond of the little beggar, you know.'

He put his hand on her arm and steered her into the kitchen before him. Scott was once again drawing large circles and lines on the newsprint, making 'Brrm, brrm' noises under his breath as the crayon swept across the picture again and again.

Lin returned to the neglected vegetables, and Soren sat at the table and talked with Scott, who had forgotten his anger with his big brother and was sunnily explaining his artwork with great seriousness.

In a lull in the conversation, Soren looked up at Lin and asked, 'Can I do anything to help?'

'No, thanks. It's all under control. I'm paid to do this.'

'Is that a dig at me? Don't add, *Mr Wingard*, will you? I might be tempted to do something about that.'

Not looking at him, she said, 'I didn't mean it that way. What are you doing here so early, anyway? I thought you'd be milking.'

'I've been made redundant. Dad reckons he wants to see if he can manage without me. They did yesterday.'

Scott picked up the sheet of paper he had been working on, and thrust it before Soren's eyes, demanding his attention. 'Hold on there, mate,' said Soren with amusement, and hauled the little boy on to his knee, spreading the drawing on the table before them, and giving it his solemn interest.

Scott wriggled down to his feet and said, 'On the wall, Sor'n. My room.'

Soren rose and said, 'Okay, feller.' He rummaged in a

drawer for some drawing pins and said to Lin, 'We're going to hang the masterpiece.'

He came back alone as Lin stood waiting for the pots on the stove to boil before turning the temperature of the hot-plates down. 'He's okay,' he said in answer to her questioning look. 'He's decided to build a city before tea. With blocks.'

Lin smiled. 'What else? Soren——?'

'Yes?' He had stopped a few feet from her, leaning against the table.

'How does it feel,' she asked curiously, 'having a half-brother young enough to be your son?'

'It feels terrific,' he said quietly.

'You're not jealous of your father's second family?'

'No. I got over all that before they had Susan. Teresa handled me beautifully. But I didn't make it easy for her.'

'I've never heard you call her that before.'

He grinned. 'The title *Ma* is a joke—sort of.'

'She told me that. I don't follow.'

'I wouldn't accept her at all, at first. I was eleven years old and I still remembered my mother. I was a brat, an only child and not willing to share my sole remaining parent with anyone, least of all his new wife. I must have made her life hell for the first few months, I know my father's patience ran out, but Teresa wouldn't let him punish me. I yelled at her that I'd never call her mother, and she said okay, I could call her what I liked as long as it was polite. So I didn't call her anything. I didn't speak to her at all. She kept on being friendly and not pushing me, and keeping the peace between my father and me. She was so damned *nice*——! I couldn't believe that a stepmother could really be so nice. I didn't want to love her. I had loved my mother and—it hurt too much when she went. So when I started softening towards Teresa, I fought it.'

'How?' Lin asked softly, as he paused and looked broodingly at the floor.

'I was a kid——' he said. 'I thought it was *her* I was fighting. I made a dirty war of it, being polite when Dad was about, and a little devil when he wasn't. She didn't tell him. I don't know how she stood it, she wasn't all that old, then, only in her mid-twenties.' His mouth twisted into a faint, wry smile. 'I thought of a marvellous insult, and called her "Old Ma Kettle" because I thought she'd hate being labelled with the name of the cantankerous old lady in the Ma and Pa Kettle films I'd seen. Before your time,' he added, looking at Lin.

'I've seen them,' she said, and laughed.

Soren nodded. 'Teresa laughed, too, when I flung it at her. And that was the final straw. I went for her physically, fists, feet and all. If my father had been there he'd have tanned the hide off me. I was a pretty wiry boy, and I must have done some damage before poor Teresa managed to subdue me. And then I saw that she was crying, and—God forgive me!—I was *glad*. Until I realised *why* she was crying. She was saying, "Oh, Soren, Soren—you poor little kid!" And she *apologised* for laughing at me. She was holding on to me like grim death to stop me fighting, but she kissed me and said she was sorry. And when I stopped trying to hit her, the hold she had on me became—an embrace.'

His voice had deepened and he wasn't looking at Lin. He paused a moment and then laughed a little. 'I just managed not to cry, myself. I thought I was a little tough guy, you know, at eleven years old. By way of apology, I said handsomely, "You're not really old." Which must have made her want to laugh again. But she didn't. She said, "Thank you. But I wouldn't mind being *your* old Ma, you know—if you'd like it.' It was a question, of course, but I wasn't quite ready to concede that much, yet. We had a sort of truce while I chewed it over, for a few days. She didn't press matters. When I finally surrendered I tried to make a joke of it—to save my juvenile pride, I guess. I remember swaggering into the kitchen and saying, "Hey, Ma! Where's my lunch?" and my father looking at me with a face like thunder for giving Teresa cheek. She stopped him with a look. I suppose she must have explained to him, later. Then she winked at me and smiled. And from then on, she was my Ma. There have been sticky patches, of course, but she's always treated me as her own. Before the others were born, she involved me with the preparation and expectation. I couldn't be jealous. Teresa spreads her love wide.'

Lin felt a tug of pain deep within her. 'You're very close to her, aren't you?' she said. 'You didn't like it when I said she was too young to be your mother. That's why you hated me, at first.'

Soren straightened away from the table and came over to her, taking her hands and looking down at them clasped in his. 'I never hated you. For a few minutes I resented the way you noticed it so quickly, that she wasn't my mother. Ridiculous—but just in those few seconds, I felt as fiercely possessive as I did twenty years ago, when I first accepted Teresa. Most people don't seem to give it a thought, and you were so positive, weren't you? It jolted me back to my childhood, and I didn't relish that. As a matter of fact, I had the distinct impression that you didn't like *me* at all.'

Lin withdrew her hands from his and turned away, lifting the lids of the saucepans on the stove and carefully turning down the heat. 'I was sorry for the girl in the post office,' she said lightly. 'I thought you were a bit of a brute to her.'

She turned back to him, smiling challengingly, and he

laughed and agreed, 'Maybe I was. I wasn't feeling very patient that day.'

'Oh—is that why you looked at *me* that way?'

Smiling, he said, 'What way?'

'As though I was something that had just crawled out from under a stone.'

His brows rose. 'I deny that!'

'All right—as though you had no time for women at all. And later you were pretty scathing about me—remember?'

'I didn't think you could do the job,' he told her. 'I pictured you running back to the city within a week, and leaving Teresa and Dad in the lurch.'

'And now?'

'I admit you've stuck it out,' he said, and his gaze suddenly became shrewd. 'I still wonder why.'

'I like it here,' she said. 'I like—your family.'

'Teresa said you told her an aunt brought you up. Do you think of her family as yours?'

'No. She was kind, but she never thought of me as her own.'

'What about your father?'

'I don't think he ever really thought of me as his own, either. My mother was the only one who really wanted me, and she died. You were lucky, having Teresa,' she added, 'I could be jealous of you.'

She *had* been jealous of him, of course. She had envied him for having Teresa, who loved him, while she had no one to replace her mother. She had childishly disliked him for having what she had always wanted, and never had.

'I know I was lucky,' Soren said. 'Teresa is one in a million. A woman of absolute integrity.'

He almost worships her! Lin thought, startled. And as she thought of her own position in this household, her heart fluttered with sudden fear. If Soren, who admired integrity so much, found out why she had come here, there could be hell to pay. She was falling in love with Soren, she might as well admit it. But if he knew the truth about her, how would he feel, then?

Susan and Tracy were deep in the throes of examination fever, scarcely putting aside their books except to eat and sleep, and the rest of the family tried sympathetically to help. They were excused from most household chores and even Davy philosophically took an extra turn at drying the dishes. Lin gave up her weekend and earned Susan's undying gratitude for her intensive coaching before the history exam. Soren had accepted her refusal, on those grounds, to go with him, but she wasn't sure how long she could continue to stall him. Their relationship had reached a stage where it must either develop or disintegrate. One was fraught with possible disaster and the other—the possibility of the other filled her with misery. In her more sensible moments she knew she must not get in any deeper, because there was no possible future for herself and Soren. But every time she saw him, sense vanished like smoke on the air. *Just let me have this*, she would think, *just a little longer to see him smile at me and listen to him teasing me and calling me Melinda in that lazy, gently mocking tone. Please—just a little while.*

The girls were too absorbed now to notice what went on about them, and Teresa was blessedly tactful, but Lin knew she was not unobservant; and Ray occasionally slanted a shrewd look at herself and Soren, though he said nothing.

Soren volunteered to help Lin and Davy with the dishes one evening, and then said to her, 'Come over to my place for a while. You look tired.'

'I am,' she admitted. 'I'd better have an early night.'

'I won't keep you up,' he promised, hanging the tea-towel on its hook by the stove. 'Davy, tell Mum and Dad that Lin's visiting me for an hour or so, will you?'

'Okay,' Davy shrugged, and lost no time scooting down the broad passageway to the sitting room and his favourite TV programme.

'I didn't say I'd come,' Lin protested feebly. 'I really am tired.'

'It's a lovely night. A short walk in the fresh air might help. And I want to talk to you.'

'What about?' she enquired cautiously.

'Must it be about anything in particular? Don't be difficult, Melinda. Just come. Please,' he added, bending briefly to brush his lips over her temple.

Weakly, she went with him. She told herself she was too tired to argue with him, but knew that was only half of it. The truth was, she wanted to be with him, more than anything. The night air was pleasantly cool, and laden with the pungent smells of the farm. He put an arm about her, drawing her under his shoulder, and said, 'Look at the stars.'

'It *is* a lovely night,' she murmured, stopping to admire the sweep of the sky, with the heavy, wanton spraying of the stars against it. But when Soren moved to bring her still closer to him, she broke away quickly and went on walking.

When they reached his cottage, he pushed open the door and turned on the light, making her blink with the sudden brightness. 'Sit down,' he said, and placed her gently on the sofa facing the small television set. 'Would you like a drink?'

'What are you offering?'

'No great choice, I'm afraid. Beer, a shandy, Coke or dry sherry.'

'Sherry, please.'

'I'll join you,' he said, and went to get it.

When he brought the glasses, he handed her one and sat down beside her, throwing one arm behind her along the back of the sofa. He raised his glass to her, smiling, and Lin smiled back and sipped the golden liquid with enjoyment. His gaze slipped over her loose shirt-blouse and hardy denim pants, and she looked down selfconsciously at her clothes and said, 'I should have changed, before I came visiting.'

'You look fantastic. You always do. I thought it was the clothes at first, but what you wear doesn't seem to make much difference.'

She said, 'Thank you,' but this was dangerous ground, and she took another gulp of her sherry, and looked away from him, fixing her eyes on the blank TV screen.

Soren said, 'Do you want it on?'

Lin hadn't been thinking of TV, just avoiding his eyes, but she said, 'Oh—I don't mind.'

He got up and switched on the set, and adjusted the controls, making the sound audible but muted. He had showered and changed before eating, and she couldn't help noticing the lithe power of the shoulders beneath his cotton knit shirt, and the long legs in snug-fitting dark pants.

She had moved further into the corner of the sofa, but when he returned to her side he sat closer to her and curved his arm about her, cupping her shoulder with his hand. For a moment she stiffened, but his arm felt friendly and warm and definitely comfortable, and she relaxed against it, pushing her conscience aside.

She drank some more sherry, her eyes on the fast-paced variety show that filled the small screen. There were dancers creating patterns with whirling skirts and flying scarves, and the effect was almost hypnotic.

Close to her ear, Soren murmured, 'Hey, you're not going to sleep, are you?'

'I could,' she said. 'Would you mind?' She smiled a little and moved her head further against his chest.

Soren took her nearly empty glass and placed it on the floor beside his own. 'Yes, I would,' he said firmly, and tipped her chin up and kissed her.

She closed her eyes and thought, *Oh, lord—this has got to stop.* But slow, delicious delight filled her as his mouth touched hers and moved softly over it, parting her lips to an insistent caress that brought a sigh from her throat into his mouth, and his kiss hardened into passion, his hand taking heavy possession of her breast.

A little scared, she moved in protest, and Soren lifted his mouth and whispered something against her throat, his lips touching her skin. His hand moved down, stroking over the curve of her waist and hip to her thigh, and she said with an effort, 'No, don't.'

Soren lifted his head to look into her half-closed eyes, his own glittering with desire. But he said quietly, 'All right.' He slid his hand beneath her thighs and lifted her legs across his knees, pushed her head to his shoulder and stroked her hair, cradling her in his arms.

Her face against his shirt, Lin murmured, 'You mustn't kiss me like that.'

'All right,' he said again. 'I won't.'

She felt his lips touch her temple, and then her cheek, then gasped as they explored the small hollow behind her ear, and the softness of her lobe. 'Nor like that,' she sighed regretfully.

His chest moved slightly in silent laughter. 'How about—like this?' he said softly, and his lips slid across her cheek to settle lightly on her mouth. Almost immediately they were withdrawn. 'Or like this?' he teased her. This time the pressure of his mouth was firmer, but equally brief, leaving her frustrated and longing for more. She made a tiny sound of protest, and he kissed her again, a butterfly touch that tantalised and irritated. He tortured her with tiny, unsatisfying kisses, saying, 'How's that,' and 'what about this?' And her voice softly clashed with his, breathless and agitated: 'Oh, stop—please—stop it——' until she could bear the sweet torment no longer, and her hand came up to hold his head and keep his lips on hers.

Soren kissed her properly, then, deeply and with devastating purpose, his hand slid inside the loose blouse and made her skin sing with desire. He pressed her back against the sofa, and her senses swam dizzily in a haze of lovely, unbelievable sensation.

She was clinging to him, holding his body against hers, knowing his urgent desire, but when at last he moved his mouth from hers, she knew the danger she was in, and some shred of sanity returned.

She gasped, 'No more, Soren!' and her hands pushed against him.

He sat up, pulling her with him in his arms, her feet swinging to the floor. 'All right,' he said. 'You don't have to fight me.'

She stopped struggling, and he stroked a strand of hair back from her face and said soothingly, 'Relax. I didn't bring you here to seduce you.'

His hold on her eased, but he kept his arm about her so that her head rested on his shoulder. 'You could have fooled me,' Lin said huskily.

Soren was laughing silently, she could feel it. 'I wouldn't dare,' he said. 'Teresa would have my hide. She looks on you as one of the family, you know. She and Dad disapprove of sex outside marriage, and they'd protect you just as they would Susan and Tracy.'

'Would they?' Lin asked. 'But *you* do as you like outside the family? The old double standard——?'

'Who said anything about a double standard?' he said coolly.

She moved her head to look up at him in surprise. He was smiling faintly, and his eyes met hers steadily. Her cheeks coloured warmly and she said, 'Oh.'

Soren laughed and she dropped her head back against his shirt. 'That seems rather—unusual these days,' she said. 'Is your father very—rigid in his views?'

'Rigid? I wouldn't call it that. He has a decided opinion and he lets it be known. He has no time for promiscuity and he doesn't distinguish between the girls and the boys. Neither does Teresa.'

'So they're in total agreement on moral standards,' she said slowly.

'Yes. It must help when people have children to bring up.'

'I suppose it must. I would have thought—Teresa would be pretty broadminded.'

'There's a difference between being broadminded about other people's morals, and adopting them yourself. I don't think she would ever condemn anyone.'

'Would Ray?'

Soren thought about that for a few moments. 'He might be a harsher judge. He can be pretty scathing about the unhappiness some people cause by being sexually greedy. He does have some justification, of course. My mother's sexual morals were anything but rigid.'

Lin stirred suddenly. 'What?'

'Don't move,' he said, his hand on her head to keep it pressed against his shoulder. 'You might as well know about it. She left here with a farm worker we had. Looking back now, I realise he wasn't her first lover. When I was a child, of course, I didn't know the significance of the assignations she used to make with men, some of them in this cottage.

She was very lovely to look at, I remember. My father didn't tell me why she left, or how. For a long time I believed she would come back. Possibly he thought so, too. When I was older I put two and two together and asked him point blank.'

'And he told you?'

'Reluctantly. He doesn't believe in lying. I'm glad he was honest with me.'

Lin moved her hand to touch his, and he clasped her fingers in his. 'I'm sorry,' she whispered. 'Do you ever see her?'

'She's dead. She moved to Wellington and her lover of the moment got drunk one night and crashed his car with her in it. She would never have come back, though. This was just a boring backwater to her—I remember how she used to complain to my father. Her marriage was a mistake, and her child was an encumbrance. If abortion had been half as easy then, I would never have been born.'

Lin winced. 'She surely didn't *tell* you that?'

'No. She shrieked it at my father once in my hearing. I don't suppose she knew I was there. Actually, most of the time she was kind to me in a slightly irritated way. Sometimes we had fun together. She was childish in many ways, she wanted to be a playmate, not a mother. Discipline bored her.'

'Did Teresa manage to impose discipline on you?' she asked.

'Yes, in her own way. Teresa doesn't drive, she leads. When she does put her foot down she does it firmly and can't be budged.'

He talked about Teresa for a while, but when she stopped asking questions he lapsed into silence, absently stroking her hair with one hand. The TV screen flickered coloured images at them, but Lin wasn't listening to the words and music that went with them, and after a while the pictures blurred and she closed her eyes. Soren's chest rose and fell evenly beneath her cheek, and the warmth of his skin through his shirt was close and comforting.

She was fast asleep and dreaming when she was vaguely conscious of being lifted in strong arms and carried, then laid gently down on a welcome softness. She murmured sleepily and was hazily aware of someone tugging at the waistband of her jeans, unfastening them and sliding them gently down over her legs. The movements briefly wakened her, and she flickered open her eyes and gasped as she saw Soren looking down at her.

'Don't worry,' he said. 'Go to sleep.' He dropped a sheet and blanket over her and repeated, 'Go to sleep.'

It seemed very odd, and she wondered if she was still dreaming. At any rate, she was too sleepy to work it out now. The bed was warm and soft, and she snuggled into it and drifted back to oblivion.

CHAPTER SIX

THE room was dim when Lin stirred again, but a brilliant sliver of light showed at the edge of the dark blind pulled down over the window. As she realised this wasn't her room, she sat up with a start, bumping her head on the wooden headboard of the bed in her haste. The exclamation she made was less of pain than of dismay that she was apparently in Soren's bed, and had been there all night.

The door was ajar, and a delicious smell of frying bacon wafted through it. She was still wearing her shirt, with some of the buttons undone, but her jeans were flung over a chair a few feet from the bed.

She had pushed back the blankets and cautiously moved to get out of the bed when there was a double tap on the door, and she hastily tucked her legs under the covers and pulled the sheet up to her waist as Soren walked into the room.

'I thought I heard something,' he said. 'Breakfast is ready. In the kitchen, or in bed?'

Lin put an agitated hand to her tousled hair and tried to smooth it back off her face. 'What am I doing here?' she demanded. 'What happened last night?'

Soren grinned and came over to the bed. He sat on it and leaned over to drop a quick kiss on her lips. 'Don't you remember?' he asked, with devilment in his eyes.

'Did you put something in my drink?'

He threw back his blond head and laughed. 'No,' he said finally. 'And nothing happened. Except that you went to sleep and I put you to bed. Disappointed?'

'Disap——? Of course I'm not *disappointed*!' she said hastily. 'But——' Her eyes went to her jeans on the chair.

His gaze followed hers and he said calmly, 'I didn't think they'd be very comfortable to sleep in. Don't look so worried. You're quite respectable underneath.'

'Were *you* disappointed?' she snapped, put out by his amused manner. 'What did you expect? Black lace?'

'I'm not at all disappointed,' he said. 'Pink cotton with white frilly bits on the edges—and very nice, too.'

Lin's cheeks flamed, and she glared at him speechlessly.

'You haven't told me where you want your breakfast,' he reminded her.

'I can't have breakfast here,' she said. 'I'm supposed to be cooking it at the house. What's the time?' she asked in sudden alarm, lifting her wrist to consult her watch. '*Oh, help!* Why didn't you wake me?'

'There's no rush,' he said.

'It's late!' she wailed. 'What on earth will Teresa and Ray think?'

'That you spent the night in my bed, of course.'

'*What?* Soren——!'

'Calm down! They know where you spent the night because I went over last night and told them. They said to let you sleep this morning. You've been working too hard and you obviously needed it.'

Suspiciously, she asked, 'What exactly did you tell them?'

'That you'd gone to sleep and I'd put you in my bed. I slept at the house last night.'

'Oh.' Lin relaxed, looking away from his quizzical expression. 'Beast! You might have told me ...'

'You hardly gave me a chance. Besides, you rise so beautifully——' He grinned and rose from his seat on the bed. 'For the third time,' he said, 'do you want a tray in bed or are you getting up?'

'I'm getting up, of course. Can I borrow a comb?'

He went to the dressing table by the window and opened a drawer, took out a small flat leather pack and extracted a tortoiseshell comb from it which he handed to her. 'Never used,' he said. 'I've put a fresh towel and face cloth in the bathroom, and a new toothbrush as well.'

'You think of everything,' she said. 'Thank you.'

He turned to go, picking up her jeans and tossing them on to the bed on his way. 'Don't be too long,' he said. 'Breakfast's getting cold.'

Some time later Lin walked into the house feeling a little apprehensive. Teresa was pouring a glass of milk for Scott in the kitchen, and she looked up and smiled at Lin, saying, 'Don't look so guilty!'

'I *feel* guilty,' Lin said ruefully. 'I'm supposed to have made breakfast, and instead, Soren has been making mine. He—said he explained to you what happened.'

'Yes, he did. And you're not to worry about it. You do more than you're paid for, Lin, and *I* feel guilty about letting you get so tired. I've been given the morning off, and I'm giving you one, too. Let's be lazy and take a couple of deckchairs out in the sun. Scotty can play outside and we'll both watch him. It just about takes two, anyway!'

Lin demurred a little, but Teresa was pleasantly adamant, and it was a lovely morning. The sun was bright and hot, the lawn dusted with tiny grey-blue butterflies hovering above the daisies, and the shrubs near the house gave hospitality to industrious bees. Scott made a complicated spaghetti network of miniature roadways in the big sandpit that Ray and Soren had made, and then climbed on the tire swing that hung from a pepper tree in the corner of the lawn, and swung sleepily back and forth, watching the grasshoppers jump along the bending blades of grass.

'I must tell Davy to mow this lawn,' Teresa murmured. 'But I rather like the daisies.' She took out a partly knitted garment from the bag at her feet and looked down at the pattern leaflet on her knees.

Lin had brought a book along from her room, but she hadn't opened it yet. They had been sitting chatting in a desultory way about nothing in particular, laughing at Scott and occasionally getting up to help him by request. Lin watched the white puffs of cloud floating aimlessly overhead and then turned her head unobtrusively so that she could see Teresa's face as the older woman bent over her knitting, her expression serene and the rhythm of her busy fingers strangely soothing.

Teresa looked up and smiled. 'Do you knit, Lin?'

Lin shook her head. 'No. My aunt did teach me, once, but I wasn't very interested. Perhaps I should take it up again.'

'You don't forget, once you've learned it. Did your aunt do much of it?'

'She always knitted when she was sitting down. She's one of those people who can't stand doing nothing. And she said knitting for the family saved a lot of money. She sewed, too—I think because she felt it was necessary rather than because she liked it.'

Teresa said, 'Soren had the idea that you were quite well off.'

In material things, perhaps, Lin thought. But she had never had it so good as Soren, with this woman as his mother, and the close-knit family she had gathered about her. 'I was never well off,' she said quietly. 'Not as well off as *your* family.'

Teresa had no idea she was being paid a compliment, and it would only embarrass her if Lin explained what she really meant. But it gave Lin pleasure, like a gift given in secret.

'We do all right,' Teresa said. 'But money isn't as important as love, is it? You haven't said much, but I've a feeling you missed out on that.'

Lin didn't answer that. She knew she didn't need to. Teresa had stopped knitting and her eyes were filled with an understanding compassion. 'It must have been hard for you, after your mother died.'

'It could have been worse,' Lin said. 'My aunt was very kind. At the time I didn't appreciate that, but she was as good to me as she knew how to be. She doesn't have a lot of imagination, that's all.'

Teresa nodded sympathetically. 'Soren lost his mother, too,' she said.

'Yes, he told me—last night.'

'You're becoming fond of Soren, aren't you, Lin?'

Lin looked up quickly, wondering if Teresa would have minded ...

'I'm fond of you all,' she said finally. 'You've been very good to me.'

'We like you, too, Lin. You've fitted in here beautifully. We'd be very sorry to lose you.'

Lin's breath seemed to stop momentarily. Was this rejection? A warning not to get too fond of Soren? Not to step out of her present role in the Wingard ménage? After all, liking the home help was quite different from accepting her as a possible future daughter-in-law. *Could* Teresa mean that? Her hands clenched tightly in her lap as she fought the tearing pain of it. When she dared to look up, Teresa looked just the same, calmly counting stitches. Her voice almost choking on the words, Lin asked, 'What do you mean, Teresa?'

Surprised, Teresa looked up. 'Well, what I said! We may

not really need a home help much longer, but we'd hate to see you go. How much did Soren tell you about his mother?'

'Everything, I think.'

Her eyes said the rest. Teresa looked back at her and said, 'Yes, I thought so. He doesn't talk about her easily, you know. When he came back here last night, I knew that—well, that you were special. I don't want to interfere, Lin, but I want my son to be happy. He *is* my son, in every way that matters, and he's taken a couple of hard knocks in his life. I think you would be good for him, and I'd like things to work out between you two, if you both feel the same way. I think you do.'

Lin couldn't deny it, and it wasn't until later that she realised with bitter self-reproach that she should have denied it and put an end to Teresa's confidences.

'I won't do any pushing one way or the other,' Teresa went on, while waves of relief washed over Lin, so that she felt faint and dizzy with it, and leaned her head against the back of the deckchair as she listened. 'The thing is,' Teresa was saying, 'neither Soren nor his father have ever been able to see his mother as a normal human being, and it colours their outlook. Especially their views on women—any women. If you can understand that, it might help you to understand Soren.'

'I thought when I first met him that he didn't like women,' Lin murmured.

'It isn't exactly dislike. But he—tends to require that they prove themselves to him. He doesn't give his trust easily. He's very demanding when he loves.'

She paused, letting her knitting drop on to her knee. 'He's like his father in many ways. More sophisticated and less innocent than Ray was before he met Soren's mother—poor Ray, he was a simple country boy, I think, although

I didn't know him then. He was absolutely dazzled. He was madly in love, and the only thing to do about that, for a young man like him, was to ask her to marry him. I don't think, somehow, that she was the tramp he thinks she was, you know, or she wouldn't have been tempted into accepting him. But she'd certainly been around a bit, and once the novelty of marriage and a quiet life on the farm wore off, she must have wanted something more out of life, I suppose. From what I've heard, she was one of those gay, irresponsible people who never grow up, who never should be allowed to hold other people's lives in their hands. I knew a man like that, once.'

Lin looked up curiously as Teresa paused abruptly, her sudden smile rueful and wistful. Then she went on, 'One should just enjoy them and let them be. They're not to be taken seriously. But it's hard not to take someone seriously when you love them . . .

'Ray was hurt, of course, when she left him, but not as deeply as Soren. Ray had seen it coming, and was probably secretly relieved, I think. He's a good man, and a strong one, in his quiet way. But she was outside his experience, he didn't know what to do with her, except retreat inside himself in dignity and not let her hurt him too much. But Soren was a child, and children have no defences. It took me a long time to get through to him.'

'He told me about it,' said Lin. 'He thinks the world of you, now.

'I know.' Teresa sounded rather dry. 'Soren sees women in two colours—black and white. And I don't mean skin colour. Oh, he'd deny it if you put it to him point blank. But subconsciously he judges all women by his own picture of his natural mother and myself. And neither picture is a true likeness. His mother *wasn't* a whore, and I'm not a saint. You know he was engaged, once?'

'Susan mentioned it.'

'Yes, well—I was a bit uneasy when he brought Sonia home and said they were going to get married. In looks she was very like his mother, and I was afraid that was the chief attraction. But he adored her. Now, I don't think that was such a good thing, but at the time I hoped it was. He thought she was perfect, and she, poor girl, tried to live up to his expectations. When he had to go overseas for several months, she promised to wait and be faithful. She waited, but she wasn't entirely faithful. If she had told him, he might have forgiven her—I don't know. But when he found out from someone else, that was the end.'

'Poor Sonia!' sighed Lin.

'Yes. I suppose, with his mother haunting his memory, it was understandable. And if she had really loved him she wouldn't have been tempted to fool around with someone else in his absence. But he was very harsh about her, and unfortunately the experience didn't add to his ability to trust in women. The thing is, Lin—with Soren, total honesty is important. If—you come to love him, never deceive him, and I don't mean just by having affairs with other men, I'm certain you wouldn't. I mean, if he found you out in deceit of any sort, it could mean serious trouble for both of you.'

Lin felt slightly sick. It wouldn't have been possible, anyway, but if she had ever been mad enough to think she might be able to get away with it, this shattered her hopes.

Teresa suddenly stood up, and Lin saw that Scott, finding a renewed fund of energy, was attempting to monkey-climb the rope of the swing. The rope swung wildly and he clung, kicked and fell.

He yelled lustily, tears streaking his face, as Teresa walked briskly to him, picked him up and inspected the damage. There was remarkably little, and after a few words of reassurance, Scott scrubbed his damp eyes with small fists and consented to another session in the sandpit, where he began bulldozing another road, with throaty bulldozer noises.

Lin was standing by her chair when Teresa walked back to her, smiling. 'He's all right,' Teresa assured her. 'No harm done.' She looked more closely at Lin. 'Are you all right? You're a bit pale—is the sun too hot?'

'No, I like it. I was a bit worried about Scott.'

'Heavens! He does that sort of thing a dozen times a week. If it bothers you that much every time, no wonder you've been feeling the strain! Here, you just sit there and I'll go and make us both a cup of tea. No—go on, I insist. That's an order.'

When she came back with the tea, Teresa began talking about something else, much to Lin's relief. She didn't feel she could have gone on discussing Soren without bursting into tears or screaming hysterically against the unfairness of it all. If she did that, Teresa would think she was mad, and perhaps change her mind about Lin's suitability as a wife for Soren.

Pain stabbed at her again, and she resolutely tried to put the tempting thought from her. One thing she could never be was Soren's wife. She must not even think of it.

She couldn't think of staying here much longer, either, and that hurt almost as much. She told herself she had always known it could only be temporary, there had never been any possibility of her staying here, but she felt she had at last found a family, and the parting would be hard.

A short while later, as they went into the house to prepare the lunch, she felt compelled to ask, 'Teresa—if I feel I can't make Soren happy, you would want me to go, wouldn't you?'

Teresa looked at her gravely. 'I think you could make

him happy, Lin, if you love him. If you feel you don't love him enough to commit yourself to him, enough to marry him, then——' She spread her hands, asking for understanding. 'I've grown fond of you, Lin. But I've loved Soren for twenty years. He's my son; I don't want him hurt again.'

'I'll try not to hurt him,' Lin murmured, picking up the cups and saucers blindly and following Teresa and Scott into the house. To herself, she demanded fiercely, What are you? A masochist? Of course Soren comes first with her! It's only right.

But the knife in her heart twisted again, and she thought, It's ironic, though . . .

It was, but Teresa didn't know that, and Lin didn't find it funny. She wanted to weep, but life went on even though her world was falling apart, and there was the lunch to be got ready.

Of course she would have to leave as soon as Ray was properly fit, and the girls had finished their exams. Until then she was needed, but after that there could be no more excuses. And in the meantime, she mustn't let Soren think she was serious about him.

That wasn't going to be easy. The safest thing to do was keep out of his way as much as possible.

She managed that for a day or two, using various excuses, and Soren didn't press her. He seemed mildly amused by her evasions, and she thought he probably imagined she was still embarrassed over his half undressing her and putting her to bed.

Each day the rural delivery van left the mail and daily paper in the box at the gate, and the men usually collected them on their way in for lunch. On the Friday following her talk with Teresa, Lin was putting the finishing touches to the table when Soren and Ray strolled in, and Ray handed her a square envelope addressed in Miss Oxford's impeccable typing. She put it by her plate to open later, and began serving the meal. Teresa, who had stayed at the house that morning, helping Lin, suddenly exclaimed in pain and dropped the knife she had been using to slice cold ham. Blood welled from a cut in her forefinger, and Lin anxiously inspected it. 'I'm all right,' said Teresa, almost snappily for her. 'I'll go and get a plaster for it from the bathroom.'

'Can you put it on yourself?' Lin asked, and Ray said, 'Let's have a look.'

'I'm all right!' Teresa protested. 'Don't fuss, Ray.' Her smile was irritated, and she pulled away from her husband's hand and hurried out of the room.

The two men exchanged a puzzled glance, then shrugged and sat down. Lin put the plate of ham on the table and took her own chair. Scott had been given an early lunch and put down for his afternoon nap, and the silence at the table was noticeable. Ray was unrolling the paper to glance at the headlines, and Soren stared with an absent frown at the doorway through which Teresa had gone, before he turned his attention to the table and began buttering a piece of bread.

When Teresa came back and seated herself, her face was serene, but Lin thought she caught a hint of underlying strain. Teresa had not really been herself this morning, she seemed tense and there was a hint of a frown between her fine eyebrows.

Ray shot her a look over the top of the paper, and returned his eyes to the print, and Lin asked in a low voice, 'Are you all right?'

'Yes, of course.' Teresa smiled at her and touched her fingers. 'You haven't opened your mail.'

Lin knew what was in the envelope, and hadn't intended

to open it at the table, but Teresa was trying to make up for her hint of irritability earlier. Lin reluctantly picked up the envelope and opened it.

The birthday card was quite ornate as cards go, pink flowers and flowing gold lettering handpainted on a white satin background. She opened it, read her father's scrawled signature and slipped the folded cheque back into the envelope. The amount would be substantial, but she wasn't anxious to know the exact figure.

Soren looked up and said, 'You didn't tell us you had a birthday coming up. When is it?'

'Today, actually. He must have posted it at the right time. It's from my father,' she added quickly, as she saw his eyebrows go up slightly.

Ray had lowered the paper and was looking over at her with a smile. 'Happy birthday, Lin,' he said. 'You should have let us know. How old are you?'

Lin hesitated, then said, 'Twenty-four.'

'Yes, of course,' said Teresa. 'You told us in your letter of application that you were twenty-three. Many happy returns, Lin dear.'

'And the same goes for me,' Soren said, smiling at her across the table.

'We must give you a party,' said Teresa, suddenly gay. 'Tomorrow. It will be a day late, but the girls can help me prepare it.'

'I wouldn't dream of putting you to so much trouble——' Lin began, but she was overruled. Teresa seemed to have shaken off whatever had been bothering her, and was happily planning. Ray approved wholeheartedly, and Soren smiled lazily and advised Lin to let Teresa have her head. 'You can't stop her,' he said. 'Don't spoil her fun.'

Later he said to her quietly, 'Would you like to celebrate quietly with me, tonight?'

Carefully she fixed a casual smile on her face before turning to face him. 'If I'm to be fresh for your mother's party tomorrow night, I think I need to conserve my energy. And I'll have to wash my hair. Thanks, all the same.'

'Not at all.' He looked at her consideringly, a slight frown in his eyes, then shrugged and turned away.

Teresa spent the afternoon telephoning prospective guests for the party—neighbours and young people of the district that Lin had met—and making a list of things needed. She and the girls went to Whakatane in the evening to take advantage of the late night shopping, and Lin put Scott to bed and went to her own room early.

She had washed her hair under the shower, and put on a light belted gown while she towelled it dry and combed it out. Then she curled up on the comfortable chair in her room and watched the television rather absently, her mind occupied by other things.

There was a tap on the door of the room, and she called, 'Come in,' wondering if the girls and Teresa were home already. It was only eight-thirty, and she had expected them to stay in the town until nine, when the shops closed.

But it was Soren who came into the room and quietly closed the door behind him.

Surprise held her still in the chair, and he walked across the carpet to stand close to her, looking down at the damp tresses over her shoulders, the drying ends curling a little about her face. She was glad she *had* washed her hair. It confirmed one of the excuses she had given for not going out with him tonight.

'What do you want?' she asked him, a little apprehensively.

He stood with his hands in his pockets, and she had to tip back her head to look at him. Perhaps he realised it was uncomfortable for her, because he moved back a couple of paces before he said, 'I wanted to tell you something.'

Her apprehension unaccountably grew, and because she was trying desperately to hide it, her voice sounded politely impersonal as she said, 'Yes?'

'I got a letter today, too. I've just been talking to my father about it. I sent my report in and asked for extended leave. I've just had the reply from my boss. They want me to go back to the Philippines for a few weeks and iron out some wrinkles that have developed, and take my leave after Christmas. I'm expected in Wellington on Monday.'

'You're going away?' she said numbly.

'I hope to be home for Christmas. Dad says he thinks they'll manage—with your help.'

'He's much better, now. Teresa isn't spending nearly so much time on the farm.'

'Will you drive me to the airport on Sunday?'

'Oh—yes, of course.' It was nearly three weeks to Christmas. She had been planning to make her own departure then, but had counted on seeing Soren every day until she had to leave. Now Soren was the one who was leaving.

'Will you miss me?' he asked quietly.

Lin gazed down at her hands, her fingers loosely intertwined in her lap. 'We'll all miss you, of course,' she said. *Keep it casual.* She must not let him know how she felt about him.

'I said, will *you* miss me?' Soren repeated deliberately.

And staring down at her fingers, she whispered, 'Yes.'

'Good!' he said very softly, and she looked up, a tiny smile on her lips, but her eyes indignant. 'Because I'm going to miss you like hell,' he added.

Her hands made an involuntary movement before she could stop herself, and Soren suddenly took a single long stride to her chair and went down on his haunches before it. She raised a hand to shield her flushed face, and said in a muffled voice, 'Soren, we don't really know each other very well. Let's not——'

As she hesitated, groping for words, he laughed a little and said mockingly, 'Let's not what? Spoil a beautiful friendship? We've never been friends.'

Troubled, she said, 'No, we haven't. Couldn't we——?'

'No.'

He sounded determined, and when she glanced at his face and saw the hard line of his taut jaw, she looked away again, biting her lip.

His hand came out and touched her face, his fingers wandering over her cheek, smoothing a strand of hair back over her ear. 'What is it that troubles you?' he asked. 'You give yourself so beautifully, and then you suddenly retreat. Just when I think we're getting close to each other, you start trying to build walls between us—invisible barriers. Why?'

His wandering hand slipped down her neck, and his fingertips slid inside the neck of her gown, exploring the line of her shoulder. She knew she should stop him, but the light touch was so tantalisingly sweet on her skin, she couldn't bear to. His eyes held hers, and he repeated softly, 'Why?'

Her lips stiff, she said, 'I—don't.'

His fingers moved down again, lightly stroking the top curve of her breast. Her eyelids flickered with pleasure and confusion, and he smiled, still holding her eyes with his. 'You do,' he said, his voice hardly more than a murmur. 'But I'm going to have those barriers down, one way or another.' Without haste his other arm came up behind her shoulders, pulling her towards him. The hand inside her gown deliberately moved until his fingers found the burgeoning centre of her breast, and she gasped, her eyes dilating, her cheeks suddenly aflame. 'Oh, don't!' she moaned, but when his lips sought hers she met them almost feverishly, her resistance melting in a sudden flame of desire.

Her arms went round his neck and clung. Soren shifted to sit on the floor, and when he pulled her from the chair to lie across his thighs, her body arched against his with no thought of denial.

When they broke apart, he was breathing rapidly, and Lin felt dizzy. In a shaking voice she said, 'You— sh-shouldn't have——'

Her face was against his shoulder, his arms still holding her trembling body. 'I had to,' he said. 'I wouldn't hurt you. You know that.'

Not deliberately, perhaps. But he didn't know what sting the bittersweet memory of his lovemaking would have, when they parted. And for him, too ...?

He stood up suddenly, pulling her with him. His hands held her shoulders, and his eyes searched hers. 'There's still something, isn't there?' he said soberly. 'We'll sort it out. At Christmas.'

Lin knew she must not be here when he returned at Christmas. She swallowed hard, trying to smile, and managed to nod, letting her head fall to rest on his shoulder. For a while they stood like that, Soren's arms holding her gently, and then he lifted her chin with his hand, dropped a swift, hard kiss on her mouth and left her.

When he had gone, Lin stood where she was for a while, bemused and fearful. What had she done? Responded to his kisses when she knew she should repulse him, shown him unmistakably that she wanted him in every way, when she had told herself she must be casual and scarcely more than friendly. And worst of all, encouraged him to look forward to seeing her on his return, when she knew it was imperative not to meet him again.

That thought was almost too much to bear, and she made a soft little sound, a whimper of pain, and threw herself on the bed, turning on her back with her hand over her eyes in a futile effort to block out tomorrow and all the bleak tomorrows that would follow.

CHAPTER SEVEN

Lin would never forget the night of her birthday party. The day had begun with drizzling rain, and the girls had sighed at the prospect of forgoing the chance for a barbecue and dancing on the newly shorn lawn. But in the afternoon the rain eased, and a watery sun gradually became strong and bright, and gilded a freshly washed garden, giving the over-abundant shrubs a softly glittering charm, and drying out the lawn so that Susan and Tracy became hopeful again.

It wasn't a formal affair, so Lin chose to wear a halter-neck sundress in white cotton sprinkled with tiny forget-me-nots, brushing her hair until it shone and leaving it loose about her shoulders. Susan and Tracy both wore jeans with loose tops, and Teresa looked both graceful and with-it in a long wrap-around batik printed skirt and white embroidered cotton blouse.

'Soren brought them home for me from his last trip overseas,' she explained, when Lin complimented her on her appearance. 'I've been too selfconscious to wear them anywhere, but this seems an appropriate occasion.'

'You look super,' Lin assured her, and Teresa said,

'Thank you. The girls said I looked okay, and that, from daughters, is the ultimate accolade!'

The barbecue had been duly set up, and Ray supervised the grilling of thick steaks and juicy lamb chops, sausages and sweet corn cobs. On the table in the kitchen nearby were bowls of salad and thick cut slices of bread, butter and seasonings, along with plates of savouries and sand-

111

wiches, with fruit salad and whipped cream for dessert.

The thirty or so guests arrived in small groups, and were soon chattering happily and laughing together. Most of them knew one another, and all had met Lin at some time since she had been living with the Wingards. She saw Rhoda and smiled at her, strolling over to join the group of young people with her, most of whom had been at the dance where Lin and Rhoda had met. A Maori boy Lin remembered from that night picked up the guitar resting on the steps behind him, struck a loud chord and began singing.

'Twenty-one today, twenty-one today——'

Lin laughed and said, 'I'm more than that! Twenty-four, actually. And it was yesterday.'

The young man grinned and said, 'Okay——

Twenty-four yesterday——'

A chorus of laughter and groans stopped him, and someone said, 'Come on, Tony, give us a proper song.'

Tony obliged with a popular ballad, and as the rest of the group joined in the chorus, Rhoda moved over to Lin's side and asked, 'Where's Soren?'

'He went back to his place to change,' Lin replied. With a pang of guilt she watched the other girl's smiling relief. If Lin had not come along, perhaps Soren would have returned Rhoda's fairly obvious feelings for him. She seemed a nice girl, and Lin had not had the right to draw Soren to herself. She remembered that at the dance she had wondered if Soren had put Rhoda up to questioning her. Now it didn't seem to matter. Perhaps he had been suspicious of her then. But they had come a long way since that night. Now she was very sure that Soren wasn't keeping Rhoda on one string while he played her on another. That sort of thing wasn't in his nature.

Well, perhaps when Soren came back from his next trip

and found Lin gone, Rhoda might have her chance. He could hardly overlook her; she was quite outstandingly lovely to look at, and not too shy to deliberately attempt to attract him. Soren might well find her attentions welcome once Lin removed herself from the scene.

It was all terribly sensible and appallingly possible, and Lin tried to be glad that things might very well work out quite nicely for Rhoda and Soren in the end. But the thought filled her with helpless, raging jealousy, and she was ashamed.

Something impelled her to turn her head, and she saw him at the edge of the splash of light made by the naked bulbs he and Davy had strung along the outside of the house that afternoon. He wore a white shirt and dark, fitting pants, and the light gave a pale glint to his hair as he stood looking for her.

She knew he was looking for her as clearly as though he called her name, and left Rhoda's side, thinking, I'm sorry—your turn may come, but tonight is mine. It isn't too much to ask, just one evening, just one sweet memory to hold through all the empty tomorrows.

He saw her coming to him, and he waited, only putting out his hands when she had nearly reached him, and taking hers.

'Hello, birthday girl,' he said, and leaned down to briefly kiss her lips. He dropped her hands to dig in his pocket, drawing out a twist of tissue paper wrapped about a small flat object. 'Your present.'

'I didn't expect a present,' Lin protested. But she opened the paper and found a beaten silver medallion on a fine silver chain, and held it to the light to admire the delicately etched Thai dancer engraved on it.

'It's lovely,' she said. 'Thank you.'

He took it from her and dropped the chain about her

neck. The small weight swung between her breasts, and Soren said, 'It looks good on you.'

It felt good, lying cool against her skin, and she smiled and thanked him, and brushed his cheek with her lips. And then he put his arm about her waist and led her over to the barbecue, where Ray was engaged in an amicable argument with Tony's father.

'Have you met Mati Hotere, Lin?' Soren asked.

She had, once or twice. He owned one of the neighbouring farms, and she recalled him coming in to see how Teresa and Ray were managing since Ray's accident.

'Course she has,' smiled Mati. 'You remember me, don't you, Lin?'

He would have been hard to forget; tall and muscular and still handsome with curly black hair peppered with grey, he had a powerful personality. He said, 'I've just been telling Ray, here, you should have put down a *hangi* for Lin's birthday, Soren.'

Ray added, 'And I've been telling Mati I'm in no shape yet for digging a pit.'

'I'd have come over and helped,' Mati protested. 'You should've sung out. Anyway, Soren here's a big strong feller.'

'The party was more or less impromptu,' Soren said. 'And it isn't just a matter of digging the pit, either. We'd have had to bring stones from somewhere, and light the fire to heat them, and put the food down hours before.'

'Too much hard work for you, eh?' Mati teased.

'You're dead right, it is,' Soren admitted cheerfully. 'Give me a barbecue, any day, if I have to do the preparation.'

'You lazy so-and-so,' Mati groaned in pretended disgust. Turning to Lin, he asked, 'Do you like *hangi* food, Lin?'

'I've never had the real thing,' she said apologetically.

'What? Hey, that's no good! You bring her over on New Year's Eve, Soren, and we'll show you how food *should* be cooked. That's the day our family has a big party. Don't forget.'

'We'll be there,' Soren promised, and somehow Lin kept on smiling. Mati turned back to Ray and began to talk about the haymaking, promising to come over with some of his boys and help out. Soren turned Lin away from the heat of the fire, and took her out on to the lawn to dance as music came floating into the night from a portable tape player set up on the back porch.

From then on, the night was theirs. They danced with their eyes on each other, and everyone else seemed to fade into the background. Between dances they strolled about, joined in the impromptu sing-songs led by Tony and his guitar, and exchanged a few lighthearted remarks with the family and their guests. But always Soren's hand was holding her fingers, or his arm lay warmly about her shoulders, and everyone smiled at them as they do at lovers. Even Rhoda managed to smile, a little wistfully, and even that couldn't dim Lin's dreaming happiness. For this night only, she was Soren's girl and everyone knew it. Lin danced with him and laughed with him, and looked at him with the tender eyes of love, and felt his touch on her hand, her arm or the smooth curve of her shoulder, with every nerve of her body.

Near midnight they dragged her forward to cut a cake with pink and white icing that the girls had made, then someone turned off some of the lights, and soon she found herself in the dark seclusion under the widespread branches of a totara, away from the noise of the party, with Soren's arms holding her close to him and his mouth demanding a passionate response from hers.

She gave it to him unstintingly, her head thrown back

against his arm, her lips parted to his sensuous exploration. She hoped the kiss would never have to end, and when it did, she stood held tightly in the circle of his arms while their breathing slowed and steadied. His lips touched her hair, and he said, 'Lin——'

Suddenly afraid of what he would say, what she would have to say, she whispered, 'Don't talk. Please don't say anything.'

He moved his cheek against her hair, and pushed a dark tress aside to kiss the curve of her shoulder.

And Teresa called Lin's name.

For a moment they both stood still and silent, then Lin stirred and said, 'Your mother wants me.'

'*I* want you,' he muttered, his mouth caressing her neck.

Teresa called again, and Soren reluctantly released her, saying quietly, 'I wouldn't let you go for anyone else.'

As she walked out of the shadow of the tree with his hand on her wrist and went towards the light, she remembered Teresa saying, *He's very demanding when he loves*. And she thought she wouldn't mind that, if only she had been allowed to love him.

Some of the guests were leaving, and Teresa had called Lin to say goodnight to them. There were one or two joking remarks made about her absence with Soren, but a look from Soren quickly quelled them.

The party broke up quite rapidly after that, and when, with the help of a few who stayed on late, they had cleared the major debris and turned out the extra lights, she felt Soren's arm come about her from behind, and his low voice said, 'I'd better say goodnight, too. Have you enjoyed your party?'

Lin closed her eyes against sudden tears, because it was over much too soon and already tomorrow had come. She could only nod in response, and he turned her in his arms and saw the shimmering in her eyes.

'What's the matter?' he asked with soft concern. And she smiled shakily and said, 'Nothing. I just can't bear it to be over.'

'Go to bed,' he said. 'You're tired.' He kissed away the tears, and when his mouth dropped lightly on to hers his lips were salty. He said, 'Goodnight, my sweet Melinda,' and pushed her gently inside to the light and the warmth and the sleepy, sated family, before he walked away from her into the dark.

When she drove him to the airport at Whakatane the following day, they spoke very little. Lin was glad that she had the driving to concentrate on, because she had to think about that, and push the thought of the fast approaching parting into the background of her mind.

It wasn't a big airfield and there were not really very many people about, but once they left the car there was no opportunity for real privacy, either. Lin felt that she should be using these final minutes to create some precious memories, but she was miserable and tongue-tied, unable to think of anything to say. When the boarding call was made, she turned blindly to Soren, seeking the comfort of his arms, and he kissed her fiercely, regardless of the stares of those about them. 'See you at Christmas,' he whispered, and Lin closed her eyes tightly so that he couldn't see the stricken misery in them.

He left her abruptly, and she opened her eyes and followed his swift walk to the plane with such intensity that they ached. He didn't turn when he reached the top of the steps, and the next moment he had disappeared inside. She watched the faces at the plane's windows, but none of them were his. She would never see him again.

Long after the plane had disappeared into the blue sky, she stood looking across the windswept grass, trying to make her mind a blank. She had to drive home, and although at the moment it didn't seem to matter if she died today, that wasn't a sane outlook. Once people were said to have died of broken hearts. Now they picked up the pieces and went on living—somehow.

If the family had been less tactful, she couldn't have borne the next two weeks. Susan and Tracy smiled knowingly when she failed to hide her unhappiness, but Ray and Teresa were simply matter-of-fact and maintained a discreet silence on the subject of their son's relationship with Lin. Of course they talked of Soren, and she listened in helpless fascination whenever his name was mentioned.

The girls, when their examinations were over, were free and delighted with their freedom, and Lin knew that her time with the Wingards must be brought to a close very soon. Teresa suggested they spend a day shopping, 'just us four women,' and leave Ray and Davy to cope with the farm and Scott. And Lin thought, *yes, I'll buy Christmas presents for them all before I tell her . . .*

She would like to do that, to give everyone something to remember her by, for a while. One day they would forget her face, her name, she would be just a girl who had once spent some time with them. But she refused to think of that.

She went shopping with them, and spent the whole of her father's generous cheque, for once getting some real pleasure out of spending his money. She bought a handsome pen set for Ray, some lovely silver filigree bracelets for the two girls, a sturdy watch for Davy, who didn't have one, and a large, indestructible metal truck for Scott. She spent a lot of time choosing Teresa's present, and settled on a carved mother-of-pearl brooch set with three small cultured pearls.

Part of the time she was with Teresa while the girls went off alone, and then Teresa and she had parted. She had to

meet them all in half an hour and there was still the most
important present to buy. She didn't have any idea what
to give to Soren.

She looked over the stock of a jeweller's and a menswear
shop without having her interest caught, then went into a
small handcraft shop and was almost immediately aware
that she had found a perfect gift. It was a small carving in
blond wood, of a bull, not the snorting, pawing angry creature of the bullring, but a great, heavy, patient, magnificent
beast like the Brahman Siddharta.

The bull was duly wrapped and paid for, and Lin
added the parcel to her other purchases and hurried off to
meet the others.

The girls were waiting for her near the huge rock at one
end of the town, that marked a spot sacred in Maori tradi-
tion that had been designated also a war memorial.

Teresa rushed along a little later, accompanied by a
middle-aged, smartly dressed woman. Both of them had
their arms full of bags and packages. 'Sorry I'm late, girls,'
Teresa said breathlessly. 'I met a very old friend. Betty and
I knew each other when we were children. I didn't know
she was living here now. Betty, my daughters, Susan and
Tracy, and our friend and helper, Lin Blake. Mrs Smeaton,
girls.'

Betty smiled at them all and then looking at Susan said,
'Hello, Lin. Now——' she smiled at the other two girls,
standing side by side. '—which one of you two is Susan,
and which is Tracy?'

Tracy smiled in an embarrassed fashion, and Susan gave
a gurgle of laughter and said, 'Actually, Mrs Smeaton,
I'm Susan. I take after my father. This is Tracy,' she
pointed. 'And this is Lin.'

Mrs Smeaton apologised, clearly surprised. 'I've never
met your father,' she said, 'But I would never have picked

you, Susan, for Teresa's daughter. You're quite different from your sister, aren't you? And yet Lin and Tracy—well, anyone would take them for sisters.'

Quite unoffended, Susan said cheerfully, 'Lin's practically one of the family, anyway.'

Lin didn't want her to expand on that, and she said hastily, 'Tracy and I have similar colouring, it makes for a sort of superficial likeness, I suppose. And Susan is definitely more like her father than her mother.'

'Now, Susan,' said Teresa, 'Can you hold some of these things for me while I write down Betty's address and phone number? You must come out to the farm and meet Ray some time,' she added to the other woman as Susan obliged, 'and see the rest of the family.'

The two women exchanged addresses and telephone numbers, and as Mrs Smeaton hurried away, Teresa said, 'Right, now—has everyone finished their shopping?'

They had, so they made for the car with their parcels, and after stopping at a supermarket for some groceries, were on their way home. Lin was quiet, brooding on the incident of Mrs Smeaton's mistake, and on Susan's casual remark and her own reaction. If she stayed much longer with the Wingards, the temptation might prove too much. Teresa and Ray liked her, and the girls would have welcomed her as a sister-in-law. She would have fitted into their family beautifully, but for one thing, the one thing that might mean disillusion and pain and heartbreak, that might shatter their warm, close family relationships and breed bitterness and accusation and rejection. She had promised herself she would never risk that happening.

The insidious voice of temptation whispered, *no one need ever know,* and she answered, *but even if I kept the secret, it might come out another way. My being part of the family must increase the danger of exposure.* Temptation

said, *How could anyone find out?* And it did seem unlikely.
But I found out, she thought. It wasn't so very difficult.

*You were looking for it—why should anyone else go
looking?*

*Yes, why should they? But supposing Teresa got curious.
Some people do. Supposing Teresa started looking—Oh,
God, if she found out that way——!*

Maybe—if I told her——

'No!'

Susan said, 'What, Lin?' and Lin realised that she had
spoken aloud.

'Nothing,' she said, and resolutely slammed the door on
hope. That had not been in the plan, and she had known
there might be temptations when she made it. And made
herself a solemn promise that no matter what happened
she would leave the Wingard home exactly as she found it.

She was guiltily aware that already she had failed in
that, that Soren, at least, was not going to accept her departure with indifference. But there was no excuse for making bad worse. And perhaps his feelings had not been as
deeply affected as hers. He had spoken no words of love,
made no commitment to her, and for that she was thank-
ful. If what he felt was no more than a strong attraction,
he would soon get over it . . .

In her room, after tea, Lin wrapped her presents in the
bright paper she had bought, and tied a gift card on to
each with a name, and 'with love from Lin' neatly printed
on each one. She hesitated over Soren's, but finally made
the message the same as for the others. It was true, after
all. But if he preferred to take it as a conventional form
of words, he could.

Later she went searching for Teresa, and told her she
was leaving before Christmas. 'You don't need me any

more,' she said. 'And—and my father will be alone over Christmas. I'm—giving a week's notice.'

Teresa was dismayed and puzzled. 'I understand you want to be with your father for Christmas,' she said. 'But there's no need to give notice. You can have the week or ten days off, of course!'

'No, that's kind, but you really don't need me,' she repeated.

'And—Soren?' Teresa asked quietly. 'He expected you to wait for him, you know.'

Once before Soren had asked a girl to wait for him, and be faithful. And she had not kept faith with him. Lin was faithful to her love, but she couldn't wait for him.

'Soren didn't say so,' she excused herself to Teresa. 'He hasn't committed himself to me, nor I to him. You said that if I couldn't make him happy——'

She stopped, because there was a harshness in her throat that wouldn't allow her to continue. She took a quick breath and added, 'I'm sorry, but I know I couldn't, and—and it's best to make a break now, before it's too late.'

Teresa looked at her gravely, and said, 'I would have thought you were wrong there, Lin. But you know your own feelings best. We'll all be very sorry to see you go. Keep in touch, won't you?'

Lin couldn't answer, because she had no intention of keeping in touch, but it would do no good to say so. She smiled mistily and said, 'I've loved being here. It wasn't only Soren, you see—it was all of you.'

Teresa said slowly, 'Yes, I think I do see. Perhaps you're wiser than I realised, Lin. You can't marry a man to gain a family—especially a man like Soren. He would have to know himself loved above all others.'

'Yes,' said Lin. That was how she did love him. She was conducting this terrible amputation more for his sake than anyone's, she realised. But the family had been a tremendous attraction, too, and it was better if Teresa thought her love had been for all of them collectively rather than Soren individually. It would stop her looking for other reasons.

Teresa tried to make it easy for her, but the leavetaking was heart-wrenching, all the same. Ray put an arm round her and squeezed her shoulder as he said goodbye, Davy scowled, the two girls hugged her and gave her a parcel labelled 'Not to be opened until Christmas' and Teresa kissed her cheek, making her eyes fill with tears. Then Scott burst into noisy crying, and while Teresa was still comforting him, Lin hastily climbed into her car and started the engine. As she changed gear at the gate and wiped tears from her cheeks, she looked in the rear vision mirror and saw them waving to her, Scott now smiling doubtfully as he fluttered his pudgy little hand. As she turned at the gateway she pinned a determined smile on her face and gave them a final wave back. Long afterwards she still carried in her mind a picture of them standing there together, watching her go out of their lives.

It was over. *Mission accomplished*, she told herself hollowly. But at a far greater cost than she had ever imagined. She couldn't say she hadn't been warned. Few of the people she contacted during the course of the search had been encouraging, and one or two had frankly disapproved and tried to dissuade her. Best let well enough alone, they said, you don't know what you might stir up that's best left undisturbed. No good will come of it, and you may make yourself and others very unhappy. Wouldn't it be better to forget the whole thing?

Would it have been better? she asked herself now.

And in her heart the answer was no. She wasn't sorry she had known the Wingards. She wasn't even sorry she had ever met Soren. She might have been saved a lot of pain, but the pain was worth what she had gained. For a little while she had known love, and if she had to pay a price for that, she was prepared to bear the cost.

The realisation lifted some of her misery and hurt, and by the time she had crossed the Rangitaiki River at Edgecumbe, on its lazy way to the sea, and driven along the flat plains road to the coast, the sight of the sea unfolding its length against a ribbon of white sand, gave her a feeling of peaceful resignation. The white cliffs, the shallow hills of the dunes, the wide Pacific, had been there for thousands of years, and would endure for thousands more. They were constantly changing and yet always remained the same. There was a kind of comfort in the thought, putting her grief into context, a brief, small personal crisis, weighed against the great tragedies of history and the cataclysmic upheavals of nature. And through all these, the hills, the sand and the sea retained their intricate, relational pattern, supremely indifferent to whatever else went on in the world.

Unfortunately the feeling didn't last, but there were times in the weeks that followed her arrival back in Auckland and her return to her father's home, when the memory of it helped her through the days.

CHAPTER EIGHT

Lin and her father spent Christmas Day with his sister and her husband. One of their children was married and living in the South Island, and the other was travelling overseas, so there were only four for Christmas dinner, and the day was a quiet one. As she thanked her aunt and uncle for the manicure set in a brown leather case they had given her, and handed them the parcel containing the Wedgwood bowl she had bought for their Christmas present, she wondered what the Wingard Christmas would be like.

Noisier, for one thing, she thought, smiling faintly. Davy wasn't a rowdy boy, but even Davy would be excited at Christmas, and Scott would show his delight with his presents in no subdued manner. She wondered what they would think of the presents she had left in her room, labelled and ready to be put under the cut pine branch that had already been brought into the sitting room and decorated before she left. She wondered if Soren had managed to get home in time for Christmas, and if he would like the carved bull as much as she had expected.

She had opened her own parcel that morning, and found not only a very pretty fringed scarf, large enough to use for a shawl, which was a joint present from Susan and Tracy, but a dainty set of pale blue lace-trimmed lingerie with a card saying, 'To our friend Lin, with love from all of us.'

She wrote a warm note of thanks to them all for the presents, mentioned that she had spent a pleasant Christmas Day at her aunt's home, and posted it after Boxing Day.

Just after New Year she cleared the post office box she had rented and found a bulky letter from Teresa, with scrawled notes from all the children thanking her for their presents; even Scott had sent his version of 'writing' on a piece of notepaper in black crayon, and Teresa had added a translation: *Scott says thank you for the truck, it's a beauty, and sends you lots of love and kisses.* Lin deciphered a crooked line of wavery x's across the centre of the page, and laughed, blinking her eyes against the sting of tears.

There was a parcel in the box, too, square and addressed to her in a firm masculine hand. Soren, of course. He must have bought her a present, and when he found her missing at Christmas, had decided to post it on. That was nice of him, and perhaps it meant he was not angry at her defection. She hoped ...

There would be a note with it, of course. It might give some indication of his feelings. But there was no note, although the indication of Soren's feelings was loud and clear. When she undid the wrapping and opened the box it contained, she found that he had sent back the little carved bull.

She didn't write to them again. Two more letters came, and she weakmindedly read them, absorbing every scrap of news Teresa gave her. She scarcely mentioned Soren, only that he had stayed home until New Year's Day and was now in Wellington. Ray was almost completely recovered, the girls had both passed their exams, and Susan would be attending university in Auckland. Lin was glad Teresa didn't hint that she might see Susan. She was tempted to write and congratulate the girls, but that would establish a link and keep the letters coming. She had de-

cided that after her brief thank you note at Christmas she
would not contact them again.

Once there was a telephone call which she answered to
hear the operator say with brisk efficiency, 'Toll's here—
Mrs Wingard calling Miss Lin Blake—is she available,
please?'

Lin stiffened. Teresa had put in a person-to-person call
to her, was waiting to speak to her. Temptation was strong,
but she quelled it.

'I'm sorry, there's no one of that name here,' she said
firmly.

The operator must have left the line open, because she
said, 'One moment, please,' and relayed the message, and
Lin flinched as Teresa's voice said, 'Never mind, cancel
it.' The operator apologised and cut Lin off.

There were no more phone calls, and the letters stopped
coming.

She was no longer working for her father, having found
a job with a travel agency. Most of what she did was routine
clerical work and making bookings, but there was a good
chance of moving eventually into the more personal side,
meeting clients and helping them to plan their itineraries.
She thought she would enjoy that.

The people she worked with were an outgoing, sociable
crowd, and she soon made friends with them. There were
occasional parties she was invited to, and she told herself
that it was only a matter of time before life would take on
new meaning, and the ghastly emptiness she felt now would
recede as she filled it with new friends and activities.

The agency was in downtown Auckland, where the green
water of the harbour could be glimpsed sometimes between
the buildings close to the waterfront, and the tang of the
sea mingled with the smells of traffic and commerce. Sometimes in her lunch hour Lin walked along the narrow

streets behind the Queen Street shops, browsing in the bookstores and buying a takeaway lunch to eat in the relative quiet of Albert Park, where the hill sloped steeply to Princes Street and the grey Gothic tower of the university.

On day in March she sat in a sheltered corner enjoying the autumnal sun, and feeding the remains of a filled bread roll to the sparrows and pigeons about her feet, when a girl's voice said, eagerly, '*Lin*! Lin, I'm so glad to see you!'

'Susan——' Lin's first emotion was of sheer joy at seeing the familiar young face. 'It's lovely to see you, too,' she said eagerly. 'Have you got time to sit and talk for a few minutes?'

'Yes, of course—I'm not due back at the university until two——'

She sat down, and Lin said, 'I never did congratulate you on passing your entrance exam. Can I do it now?'

'Never too late,' Susan grinned.

'How is university life?'

A faint shadow crossed the younger girl's face. 'It's all right,' she said. 'I suppose I'll enjoy it once I get used to things. I miss home, though.'

'Where are you living?' Lin asked.

'Oh, I'm boarding with an old couple—well, they're not *terribly* old, but older than Mum and Dad. It's rather —quiet. I think I would have liked to be in a hostel, but they were all full up.'

'Have you made any friends?'

'Sort of.' Susan shrugged. 'Only Mr and Mrs Hardwick don't like me taking friends home to their place, and they're a bit sticky if I want to stay out late. I don't think they really trust young people.'

She looked down at her hands, an unaccustomed droop to her mouth, and Lin experienced a piercing sympathy.

The normally ebullient Susan was strangely subdued and vulnerable, trying to find her feet in a new environment.

Gently, Lin said, 'Well, you haven't had long yet to settle in, have you? Are you finding the work hard?'

'Some of it. Some isn't as bad as I expected, actually. Lin, why don't we——?' But the quick light in her face suddenly died, and she muttered, 'I mean—oh, never mind.' She stood up suddenly and said with a heartbreaking effort at a gay smile, 'Well, it's been super talking to you, Lin. I'll tell the family I met you. They'll be glad to hear you're okay. You *are*, aren't you?'

Lin couldn't bear it. Susan was lonely and lost and hurt, and she had obviously just recalled the unanswered letters and the refused phone call. She thought Lin was finding her a nuisance and wouldn't want to see her again.

Lin stood up, too, catching at the girl's arm. 'Wait, Susan,' she said. 'Are you free at this time tomorrow? Maybe we could have lunch together—please?'

This time the smile was genuine and dazzling. 'Oh, that would be *super*, Lin! Shall I meet you here?'

Lin couldn't be sorry that she had weakened. She would never have forgiven herself if she had let Susan walk away, and ignored her plight. In a few weeks, a couple of months, the girl would find other friends and regain her shaken self-confidence. Then Lin could quietly ease out of her life again, without being missed too much, but right now she was needed, and she couldn't turn her back on that.

They lunched together quite often, in the park if it was fine, but more often in one of the lunch bars or coffee bars where Lin would insist on 'shouting' Susan a meal, saying, 'I'm a working girl, so I can afford it, honestly. You're only an impecunious student, my girl. From all accounts most of you are half starved.'

'I'm not!' Susan grinned. 'One thing about Mrs Hardwick, she certainly feeds me. In fact, I'm probably getting fat.'

Lin met the Hardwicks one Sunday when she called to collect Susan for a drive around the city. They seemed very respectable and slightly dour, and Mrs Hardwick asked some sharp questions about how and when she had met their young boarder and what they intended to do with the afternoon. Lin's answers appeared to satisfy her, and she even relented to the point of asking Lin if she would care to stay for tea with them when she brought Susan back.

Biting back laughter at the comic astonishment on Susan's face, Lin accepted the invitation.

As they drove away from the house, Susan looked at Lin with awe. 'Mrs Hardwick's taken a fancy to you,' she said. 'I nearly dropped when she invited you to tea.'

'She sees me as a steadying influence, I think,' Lin laughed. 'A sober and sensible older friend to keep you out of mischief.'

Susan gurgled. 'Sober and respectable—it makes you sound ancient! Where are you going to take me, *Auntie Melinda*?'

'We're going to do the grand tour of Auckland. Monuments and points of interest, and I expect you to remember all the relevant facts,' Lin said with mock severity. 'Perhaps you should take notes ...'

'That'll be the day! I do enough of that on weekdays.'

Lin drove slowly through the Domain which surrounded the imposing War Memorial Museum, and they climbed the steps outside the building to admire the view of the harbour and the volcanic island of Rangitoto rising gently from the water. A stiff breeze drove them inside to have a couple of happy hours wandering among the exhibits, paying particular attention to the replica of a nineteenth-century street, which was Lin's favourite section, and the long Maori war canoe and carved meeting house which fascinated Susan.

'You haven't seen all of it,' said Lin, as they emerged into the fitful sunlight. 'But it can get very tiring trying to cover it all in one afternoon. You can come back another time.' They returned to the car and drove to the top of Mount Eden, one of the city's many volcanic cones. The view from there was extensive over the city and the harbour, but the wind was decidedly fresh, and they didn't linger. At the foot of the hill they visited the beautifully laid out gardens which had transformed the ugly scar of a disused quarry into a small area of charm and restful interest. At Parnell they strolled around the rose gardens, admiring the blooms and enjoying the pervading rose petal scent, then window-shopped in the restored nineteenth-century shopping area on Parnell Road. Then before returning to the Hardwicks' they drove along the waterfront as far as Mission Bay, where a few hardy swimmers splashed about in the sea and people played and strolled with children and dogs on the neat grass or the cool white sand.

Lin parked the car for a while, and they took off their shoes and paddled in the wavelets that rippled to the shore, then walked across the grass to admire the fountain. Sitting on its rim with her fingers idly dabbling in the water, Susan said, 'Mum says I shouldn't mention it, but —Lin, why didn't you write to us? I mean, after that one letter you sent us—nothing!'

Caught unawares, Lin said lightly, 'I'm afraid I've never been much of a letter writer. Some people aren't, you know.'

Susan flushed and said, 'I'm sorry, I should have kept my mouth shut.'

Lin was sorry, too. She should have known Susan wasn't to be fooled by such an obvious excuse.

'It's all right, Susan,' she said. 'I didn't realise you would mind so much.'

'We liked you. And we thought—well, Tracy and I thought——' She stopped, chewing on her lip, and blurted out, 'Soren thought you'd be there at Christmas.'

Lin paled a little. 'I'm sorry if he was—disappointed,' she said evenly. 'But I'm not responsible to Soren, you know.'

Susan's brow wrinkled. 'No, but—Lin, you didn't have a row, did you?'

'No.'

'At your party——' Susan hesitated and looked at Lin in perplexity.

'Oh, Susan!' Lin said, smiling. 'People can't be held to account for what happens at parties, you know.'

Susan said gravely, 'Can't they?'

Lin bit her lip, and laid an apologetic hand on Susan's arm. She should have remembered that Susan was a Wingard. Her effervescent personality didn't denote silliness; there was a strong core of integrity and strength of character she had inherited from her parents.

'You don't understand,' said Lin. 'But believe me, I couldn't have acted any differently. Come on, we'll be late, and I'm sure your landlady wouldn't approve of that.'

They were not late, and Mrs Hardwick served them with a satisfying though slightly unimaginative meal of cold corned beef with potatoes and a lettuce salad. Her husband ate his with quiet concentration, hardly lifting his eyes from his plate, and Mrs Hardwick asked what they had done with the afternoon and listened without comment to Susan's description of what she had seen. Afterwards the two girls did the dishes, and Mrs Hardwick gave permission, with a hard stare at them both, for Susan to take Lin to her own bedroom while Mr and Mrs Hardwick watched the news on the television. 'But she's not to stay late, mind,' the woman warned.

Susan flushed, raising her eyes to the ceiling as she moved out of the sitting room doorway, but Lin smiled and assured Mrs Hardwick she wouldn't stay long. She was sorry for Susan. The Hardwicks would look after her almost too well, but their rather repressive régime would be hard for a girl of her character to tolerate.

She left well before nine, Susan seeing her off from the front gate. The subject of Soren had been tacitly avoided for the remainder of the evening, but as she drove back to her father's home, Lin was haunted by thoughts of him. Susan had implied that her departure had disappointed him, and she had had to bite back a string of questions— was he very upset? How had he reacted? Had he been angry?

He must have been angry, to send back her present to him without a word. He had probably decided to put her right out of his mind, and he was probably determined enough to do it. In anger he was ruthless. He had broken his engagement without compunction, as far as she could gather. He didn't forgive easily.

The carved bull stood on the small table beside her bed, now. It was there when she woke in the morning and when she switched off the light before going to sleep, and when she looked at it she could remember every detail of the day Soren had walked with her and laughed with her, and introduced her to Caesar and Siddharta.

The next time she saw Susan, on a day of intermittent rain and a cold wind that blew droplets from the branches of the trees in the park on unwary pedestrians, the younger girl flew down one of the steep, damp paths with a speed that made Lin afraid for her safety. She came to a breathless stop as Lin called in alarm, 'Do be careful, Susan! Those paths are slippery in the rain.'

'Hello, Lin. Guess what?'

'Something good?' Lin laughed, seeing the sparkle in the other girl's eyes and the wide, excited smile.

'You remember Rhoda Moers, don't you?'

Lin's heart plunged suddenly, picturing Rhoda, lovely blonde Rhoda, engaged to Soren. Her lips smiled stiffly and she nodded, unable to muster words for a reply.

'Well, she's back in Auckland, and she's got a flat, and she wants me to share with her. Isn't that super? I asked Mum and Dad, and they said it's okay. They know Rhoda and she's nice. They even said they'd help me with my share of the rent. I'm moving in next week.'

Relief made Lin almost dizzy. 'That's marvellous,' she managed to say, eventually. 'You'll be much happier. The Hardwicks are the salt of the earth, but not really your kind of people, are they?'

'You bet they're not!' Susan agreed feelingly. 'I know they're awfully *good*, but they make me feel sort of—sort of——'

'Inhibited?'

'Yes! That's exactly it. By the way, we're going to have a flatwarming just about as soon as I move in. You will come, won't you?'

'Oh, I don't think——' Lin demurred.

Susan's face showed her dismay. 'Oh, but can't you come? We haven't definitely decided on the date, though we thought Saturday. We can make it another night——'

'Just for me? You couldn't——'

'Yes, we could, Rhoda won't mind.'

'Look, Susan, I'm not sure if Rhoda will want me at her party——'

'Oh, *Lin*! That's crazy! Of course she wants you. She specially asked me to make sure you could come, and she said to tell you if you want to bring along a boy-friend, that's fine.'

'Are you sure——'

'I'm sure,' said Susan. 'So you're coming. Aren't you?' she demanded.

'Well, all right.' Lin didn't know why Rhoda should be so insistent on having her at their flatwarming, but perhaps it was for Susan's sake. Lin didn't have a boy-friend, though she knew one or two men she could ask to accompany her to a party. Maybe Rhoda was hoping she would turn up with a man, showing that she had no further interest in Soren.

She didn't take a man to the party. One of those she had in mind had to go to a conference that weekend, and the other, she remembered, was terribly susceptible to pretty blondes. He would probably take one look at Rhoda and spend the rest of the evening figuratively at her feet. Which wouldn't do much for the supposition that he was Lin's boy-friend.

The dress she chose was a deep burgundy velvet, with long fitting sleeves and a vaguely mediaeval look, enhanced by a plaited belt laced with gold thread and tied loosely on the hips. The neckline was low and wide, and needed something to fill it in. She put on Soren's silver medallion, but the silver was wrong with the gold in the belt of the dress, and besides, Rhoda probably knew that Soren had given it to her.

She opened her drawer and took out her father's Christmas present, a gold link necklace with a pendant of gold wrought in the outline shape of a heart, with a large tear-shaped garnet hanging inside the heart.

She put it on, and it went perfectly with the dress. She had wondered at her father choosing something as sentimental as a heart, but when she thanked him for it, he said, 'Miss Oxford said you'd like it.'

Lin gathered that Miss Oxford had been delegated to buy her Christmas present, and her initial pleasure in its beauty vanished. She had suppressed a sudden savage desire to ask him how the hell Miss Oxford could possibly know what she would like, and said in a colourless voice, 'It's very nice.'

She snuggled into a jacket of fake fur, because winter was on its way and the night air was chilly. Her father would have bought her real furs, but she was adamant about not accepting them. The thought of wearing the skins of dead animals made her shudder, beautiful though they were.

Her father scarcely glanced up from his paper when she said goodbye. He did ask, 'Where are you going?' and she told him to a friend's flatwarming party, but she doubted if he would remember five minutes after she had left. He would probably have gone to bed by the time she came home. She was tempted to stay home and keep him company, since tonight he didn't seem to be working, but she had found that his idea of relaxing was to switch on the television and not have to concentrate. He had enough 'natter', as he called it, around him at the office, and conversation with his daughter bored and annoyed him.

Lin had no trouble finding the flat, and though there were several cars parked outside it wasn't difficult to find a place for hers under a street lamp.

She could hear music and muted talk as she rang the

door bell, and then Susan flung open the door and brought her into the lighted, noisy warmth. Susan was looking very grown-up in black velvet pants and a white silk shirt, but her wide smile was the same as ever.

'I'll take that into the bedroom for you,' she offered, as Lin removed the fake fur. 'It's gorgeous! Is it real?'

Lin shook her head. 'I wouldn't wear it. You look very sophisticated.'

Immediately spoiling the image with a schoolgirl giggle, Susan said, 'Do I? Rhoda lent me the blouse, and she put my make-up on.'

Lin looked round the room, seeing what seemed to be quite a crowd of people, and saw Rhoda coming towards them as Susan stepped aside to let Lin move forward. And behind Rhoda, holding a glass in one hand, the other thrust indolently into a pocket, his green eyes frostily looking her over, was Soren.

Rhoda had reached her, and she was still staring at Soren over the other girl's shoulder, but he hadn't moved.

Vaguely she heard Rhoda greeting her, and saw that she was smiling, and somehow she forced her own facial muscles to move into some semblance of an answering smile. She said hello to Rhoda, wrenching her eyes away from Soren, and as Susan repeated her intention of taking the fur jacket to the bedroom, Lin said, 'I thought Soren was in Wellington, Susan.'

Susan looked embarrassed and apologetic and hopeful all at once, and said, 'Well, he was. He just arrived today, actually. It's a lovely surprise, isn't it?'

She looked anxious and pleading, now, and if she had planned the lovely surprise for Lin's benefit, she was obviously wondering if it had been a horrible mistake.

Lin swallowed and said, 'Yes, lovely.'

Susan looked relieved, and Rhoda took her arm and said,

'Come on, Lin. I'll introduce you to the others.'

There were only about a dozen people in all, but Lin couldn't have remembered any of their names five seconds later. Her whole attention was concentrated on the tall man who stood against one of the windows and hadn't moved since she came into the room. Rhoda said, 'And of course you know Soren,' and Lin made a tremendous effort, looked straight into his enigmatic eyes and smiled. 'Yes, of course,' she said.

There was no smile on his face for her. He gave her a cool, bored nod, then Rhoda said, 'Soren, would you get Lin a drink, please? There's someone else at the door——'

He moved over to Lin with controlled male grace and said, 'What will you have, Melinda?'

Her eyelids flickered at the remembered inflection of his voice saying her name. The familiar mockery seemed to have intensified, and acquired an edge. She said the first thing that came into her head. 'Gin and tonic, if there is any.'

'We'll see, shall we?' He took her arm, his fingers just barely touching the velvet sleeve, and she felt the touch like a brand against bare skin. He led her to a small table crowded with bottles and glasses, and poured her drink, and she said, 'Thank you,' and looked about for somewhere to sit.

There wasn't a vacant chair, and someone else came to the improvised bar, forcing them to move out of the way. Soren drew her over to a corner by a bookcase, and leaned his arm against the wall, so that he blocked her view of the rest of the room, and isolated the two of them in the corner.

Nervously Lin sipped at her drink, and Soren asked, 'And what have you been doing with yourself since you left us?'

Trying to appear casual, she shrugged. 'Working, mostly.'

'You—work?'

'Of course I do!'

'Where?'

Cautiously, she said, 'A travel agency, in town.'

'That's what Susan told me,' he said. 'She didn't seem to know where, though. Or which agency.'

Lin had never told her. And she wasn't telling Soren, either. She shrugged again, and said, 'She never asked,' and before he could ask, himself, added hastily, 'I was told you were in Wellington. What are you doing in Auckland?'

'Do you care?'

She looked down at her glass and said stiffly, 'I was just making conversation.'

Soren took a sip from his glass, not taking his eyes from her. When he lowered the glass, his eyes lowered, too, playing over the neckline of her dress and the garnet pendant. Nervously she put up a hand and closed her fingers about the gold heart. And Soren said, 'That's nice. Another gift?'

'What?' She dropped her hand quickly, her eyes puzzled and wary. The pendant swung back against her skin, the jewel in the centre still moving slightly, catching points of light.

'This,' said Soren, slipping his fingers under it, against her skin, and examining the stone, turning it a little to see it better. 'Is it a gift, like your wrist watch and your car?'

'It was a Christmas present,' she said jerkily. 'This is the first time I've worn it.' She almost shuddered with relief as the disturbing warmth of his fingers was withdrawn, and the heart dropped once more back into place.

Lin remembered the little carved bull standing on her bedside table, and couldn't resist asking, 'Why did you send back my present to you?'

He straightened away from the wall, and finished his drink before he answered her. 'I didn't want any reminders of you,' he said.

With an effort she managed not to wince, because his voice was suddenly harsh and wounding.

Almost in a whisper, she said, 'Please don't hate me, Soren.'

He turned to place his empty glass on the nearby table and then he faced her again, his head tipped consideringly, his eyes hard and contemptuous. 'Hate you?' he echoed, with steely amusement. 'My dear girl, if you're not worth loving—and you're not—then you're certainly not worth hating.'

It hurt, more than she could have believed possible. She pressed against the wall, as though Soren threatened her and as though it might be possible to get away from the hurt. She moved her head rather pathetically in negation, but his hard expression didn't alter. She realised that her hand was shaking, the liquid in her glass scintillating with its involuntary movement, and she blindly raised the glass to her lips and tipped a gulp of liquid down her throat.

It steadied her a little, and she pulled herself together. 'I don't think we have anything more to say to each other, do you?' she suggested composedly, and tried to edge around him, holding her head high.

But his hand was on her arm again, this time gripping almost painfully. With quiet menace, he said, 'I have plenty to say to you, now that you're here. Don't go away yet.'

The room had rapidly filled with people, and the babel of noise had grown considerably. Two couples were dancing in the centre of the floor, and several people sat on cushions thrown down on the carpet. Rhoda was talking to a young man wearing a bemused expression, and glasses which he kept adjusting as though he couldn't believe they weren't distorting his vision, and Susan was letting in some more people at the door.

Stubbornly, Lin tried to ease her arm from Soren's hold, her eyes holding his defiantly. 'I want to join the party,' she said.

His grim mouth suddenly smiled, but his eyes remained cold. 'Okay,' he said. 'Let's do that.'

He swung her into the centre of the floor before she could protest, and pulled her close to dance with him. It wasn't what she had meant, and he knew it. But short of making a scene, she had no choice. And he knew that, too.

She tried to move away and dance less intimately, and for a few seconds Soren let her, but there were more people wanting to dance, and there was very little room. Some were dancing apart, but there wasn't really enough space and they gave up.

When the music stopped and someone went over to the player to change the tape, Lin moved out of Soren's arms and left the floor, but he was right behind her, and from then on the party became a sort of dreadful parody of her birthday party at Paikea. His arm was about her waist and his fingers spread possessively over her midriff. When another couple smiled at them and began a friendly conversation, Soren leaned against the wall near them, and shifted her in front of him, holding her easily against his body with an apparently casual but virtually unbreakable embrace, his hands linked in front of her. Lin gritted her teeth and smiled at the other man and his girl-friend, who had their arms about each other affectionately. And her hand slid secretly into Soren's sleeve above the wrist and she dug her fingernails into his flesh.

She felt the swift intake of his breath, but he barely faltered in what he was saying to the other man. But his fingers moved slightly and gave her waist a sharp, painful nip. Then he said, 'Come on, Melinda, let's dance.'

He propelled her back to the floor and she gave in and danced again. Lin wouldn't have spoiled Susan's party for anything, but she was counting the hours and minutes until she could leave without causing comment. She danced stiffly at first, but the music was hypnotic, and for a few minutes she closed her eyes and relaxed against Soren's taut body, pretending she was back in Paikea and the party was the one Teresa had given for her.

Whenever Susan caught sight of them, she beamed approval, and Lin was torn between laughter and tears. Rhoda seemed the continual centre of an admiring circle of men, and Lin never managed to catch her eye. Once she said uneasily to Soren, 'Shouldn't you be paying some attention to Rhoda?'

He looked over to where Rhoda was and said, 'She's getting plenty of attention.'

She couldn't argue with that.

When the two hostesses began passing round plates of savouries and sandwiches, she managed to escape Soren for a while, going into the kitchen and insisting on being of some help. She glanced rather anxiously at Rhoda, but the girl seemed as friendly and placid as ever; either she didn't care that Lin seemed to be monopolising Soren, or she was too proud to show it. Soren seemed to have disappeared for a short time, but after the supper had been cleared away Lin came out of the kitchen to see Rhoda accost him with a hand on his arm and her pretty mouth lifted to whisper something to him.

Soren grinned and dropped an arm about the girl's shoulders, his eyes scanning the room until he found Lin standing in the kitchen doorway. Then he pulled Rhoda into the centre of the floor and began to dance with her.

Another man approached Lin, and after a moment's

hesitation she danced with him, and after that found herself dancing with several successive partners. Soren changed partners once and then returned to Rhoda, she noticed. And Rhoda laughed and chattered happily with him, her lovely face aglow.

As soon as one or two people made a move to leave, Lin followed suit, quietly cornering Susan and telling her she must be on her way.

'Meet me for lunch on Monday?' Susan said eagerly. 'It's a super party, isn't it?'

'Super,' Lin agreed. Susan would want to talk about it on Monday, of course. She was tempted to invent some other engagement, but it would only put off the discussion to a later date, so she said, 'Okay, lunch on Monday.'

The night air was cool, and at first she thought that was the reason the car wouldn't start. When she finally gave up and looked about for a telephone box, there wasn't one in sight.

She looked up at the window of the flat, the only one about with a light showing, and reluctantly went back into the building.

Rhoda opened the door, and Susan came up behind her, her face a study in surprise. 'My car won't start,' Lin explained. 'I'd better phone for a taxi.'

'We don't have a phone yet,' Rhoda told her. 'Maybe one of the boys could fix the car for you——'

'I wouldn't want to take anyone away from the party,' Lin began, when Soren strolled over, resting his hand lightly on his sister's shoulder. 'Trouble?' he enquired politely.

Susan explained, and he said, 'I'll run you home.'

'No!' Her refusal was instant and, she realised, too abrupt. Catching the two girls' surprised glances, she stammered, 'I don't want to trouble you, Soren. Thank you, but——'

Smoothly, he said, 'It's no trouble. I have a car here.' He took the keys from his pocket, and Susan said, 'Soren will look after you, Lin.'

He put his hand on her waist and almost pushed her out of the door. She didn't dare to look at poor Rhoda as the door closed behind them.

CHAPTER NINE

Soren almost thrust her into the passenger seat of a car, and as he slid in beside her asked curtly, 'Where to?'

Reluctantly, she told him, 'Remuera.'

His eyebrows rose slightly, but he said nothing. Well, too bad if it surprised him. Her father liked living in the old but prestigious suburb, and she didn't have to explain anything to Soren.

There were few other cars about, but he drove quite slowly, taking his time. He seemed to know Auckland, she thought, finding his way across the city without any hesitation. The car was unfamiliar, and she asked, 'Have you bought a new car?'

'Mine is still at Paikea,' he said. 'I have the use of this while I'm in Auckland.'

She presumed it was a Departmental vehicle, and since his tone didn't encourage conversation, she lapsed into silence.

He didn't speak until they turned into Remuera Road, when he asked, 'Which way?'

'Right,' she told him. 'And then the fourth street on the left.'

When he turned into the fourth street and drew the car to a halt in the shadow of one of the plane trees that lined it, she felt every nerve suddenly tingle with apprehension. Her chin went up as she turned to him.

'We're not there yet,' she said.

'I know.' His voice was hard. 'I want to talk to you.'

'You've had all evening——'

'Alone,' he interrupted ruthlessly. Then softly he added, 'Just the two of us.'

Suddenly inexplicably frightened, Lin protested, 'It's late, and I'm tired. Don't you think——'

'No, I don't——' Soren said forcefully, and suddenly leaned over her to snick the lock on her door. 'I've done enough thinking since Christmas. Now we're going to talk.'

He unlocked both their safety belts as he moved back into his seat, with one arm still on the seat back behind her head. 'Shall we have a little light on the subject?' he suggested quite pleasantly. But when he raised his hand and switched on the interior light, Lin blinked, not only because of the sudden glare. His face looked harsh, all planes and shadows, and as she met the narrow glitter of his eyes she instinctively made a tiny, futile movement of withdrawal.

He sat facing her, his right arm resting on the rim of the steering wheel, and she felt trapped. Nervously she said, 'I don't think we have anything to talk about, Soren.'

'Don't you?' he asked with savage derision. 'How about telling me why you left, for a start? That should start the conversational ball rolling.'

'I wasn't needed any more. You know Ray was quite fit even before you went to Wellington. The job had come to an end.'

'You were expected to stay until after Christmas. You didn't say anything to me about leaving before then—nor to anyone else, until after I'd gone.'

'I gave Teresa a week's notice.'

'*Notice!*' He checked himself, then said coldly, 'Do you seriously want me to believe it was just a job to you, that Teresa was nothing more than an employer?'

'It was a very pleasant job,' she said quite steadily. 'And

Teresa was a particularly—considerate employer.'

'And that's all?'

That was far from all, but that was the way she had decided to leave things, and she had to stick to it. 'Yes,' she said. 'What else?'

His look was piercing, but she managed somehow to meet it with a semblance of polite indifference.

'You know,' he said, rather slowly, 'she was quite fond of you. Would it have been so hard for you to write a letter now and then?'

'I'm not a great letter writer,' she shrugged. 'I'm sure she understands.'

'Are you? I'm not. I'm sure she's hurt.'

Lin looked away, reminding herself that he didn't know how cruel he was being.

'Then I'm sorry,' she said, 'but I can't help it.'

Flatly, he said, 'You unfeeling little bitch!'

Lin bit hard on her lower lip to stop a gasp of pain. She couldn't take much more of this, she thought with desperation. 'Are you going to take me home?' she asked him. 'Or shall I walk the rest of the way?'

'I'll take you when I'm good and ready,' he said savagely.

Anger stirred, and she turned to fumble at the unfamiliar lock, determined to get out and find her own way home.

When Soren pulled her hand away from the door, she raised the other one and tried to push at him, and there ensued a silent, undignified and finally painful little struggle that ended with both her wrists held tightly in one of his hands while he leaned over her shoulder to snick down the lock again.

She shook tumbled hair out of her eyes and glared at him, realising how close he was as she caught the clean male scent of his skin. She realised, too, that he had gained some grim masculine satisfaction out of his victory, and she made another hopeless effort to free herself. His grip tightened until she thought her bones would crack, and she gasped, 'You're hurting!'

'It hurts because you're fighting me,' he said. But his fingers relaxed just a fraction as he added, 'Just keep still and make up your mind that you're not going anywhere yet. I haven't finished with you.'

'What do you want?' she demanded.

His eyes glinted down at her and he said softly, 'Now that's a leading question.' One long finger brushed back a strand of hair from her cheek, and she jerked her head away to avoid his touch. It was too searingly familiar and too frighteningly desired.

Soren was sitting very still, but she knew he was staring hard at her averted profile.

'Teresa got one letter, at least,' he said. 'You didn't even leave me a note.'

'Should I have?' she asked, her voice strained.

'Yes, you should. I was entitled to that, at least.'

'You had no rights over me, Soren.'

His hands moved to grip her shoulders through the thickness of the fur that covered them, and he turned her to face him. 'I'm not talking about rights,' he said harshly. 'But you owe me an explanation, and you know it. Or do you make a habit of making love to men and then leaving them flat without a word?'

Her lips parted on a hot denial, but her brain checked her. She must persuade him that she hadn't cared for him, and he had given her the cue.

'A few kisses?' she said, trying to sound slightly amused as well as indignant. 'Good heavens, Soren! You're not the only man I've kissed, you know!'

That got to him. She could see the shock of it in the

sudden total lack of expression in his face. The grip on her shoulders tightened until she almost cried out, and then suddenly she was free. The fur slipped a little as he almost thrust her from him. His voice was almost expressionless, too, as he said, 'Just tell me one thing. Did you come back to Auckland because there was a man here waiting for you?'

'I told Teresa——'

'I know what you told Ma,' he said, and Lin experienced a sudden, hysterical desire to laugh at his incongruous use of the nickname. But he went on, 'If there was any truth in that, you'd have told me the same thing in the first place. It wasn't your father you wanted to spend your Christmas with. *Was* it another man?'

She couldn't bring herself to say yes, and yet if she said no it was a way of leading him on, and she daren't do that. She pulled the fur about her tightly and said, 'It isn't any of your business, Soren. Will you please stop this inquisition, and take me home?'

His right hand suddenly clenched into a fist and he raised it and brought it down hard on the rim of the steering wheel. Lin winced and sat very still, her heart thumping.

Then, without a word, Soren shifted in his seat and turned on the ignition, reaching up with the other hand to snap out the light.

He drove on down the street, and she directed him quietly to another left turn, then said, 'This will do, thank you.'

He stopped but left the engine running, and asked, peering out into the darkness, 'Is this where you live?'

'Near enough,' she said vaguely, and made to open the door.

Soren said, 'I'll see you to the door.'

'There's no need.'

'I'll see you to the door. So this had better be where you live, because I'm not leaving until you're safely inside.'

Lin bit her lip, hesitating, then finally gave in. She sat back in her seat and said resentfully, 'Half way down the street. The white stone building with the three letter-boxes.'

A few seconds later he drew up again, and this time switched off the engine.

Lin said, 'Thank you for the lift,' and turned to open the door. He leaned over her and did it for her, but he kept his fingers on the handle, instead of pushing the door wide, and as she looked up in an automatic questioning, he said, 'What's one kiss more or less?' and his lips found hers and pressed her head back against his arm that lay along the back of the seat.

Lin remained passive under the kiss, fighting wild desire that urged her to put her arms about his neck and return it passionately; until his hand moved to her shoulder to pull her closer, and his mouth hardened on hers, seeking a response she dared not give. She clenched her hands and pushed against his chest, and after a long, struggling moment Soren released her.

She pushed open the door and got out, and he slid out behind her. 'I'll be all right now,' she said. But without a word, he put a hand on her arm, and accompanied her up the path to the door. A light showed dimly through the glass upper half of the door, and as she fumbled for her keys and found the house key on the ring he asked, 'Is your flatmate still up?'

Her father had either got out some paperwork, or dozed off in front of the TV, but even as she opened her mouth to explain, she checked herself. Soren evidently assumed she was flatting with another girl, and if she mentioned her father he was quite capable of insisting on meeting him.

And if he met her father, he might ask some pertinent questions. She wouldn't put it past him.

'Oh, I don't think so,' she said jerkily. 'It's quite late. Perhaps she forgot to turn the light off.'

'If your car keys are on that ring,' he said, 'give them to me, and I'll bring back your car tomorrow morning.'

'Thank you, but there's no need.' She inserted the key in the lock and pushed the door ajar. And as she withdrew it, Soren took the ring from her and, finding her car keys, began to draw them from the ring. 'I said there's no need!' Lin repeated.

'Yes, there is.' He pulled the keys off and handed the ring back to her.

'I'll send someone round from the garage,' she said. 'They can fix it and return it to me.'

'I'll do that. Don't argue. It's a matter of conscience, and anyway, they wouldn't get far without the rotor arm.'

'The—what?' She didn't know a great deal about engines, but she had a pretty good idea that removing the rotor arm was the classic way to immobilise a vehicle.

'I took it out,' he said calmly.

'You—*what*?'

'I told you I wanted to talk to you,' he said, ignoring the rising indignation of her voice.

'You've got a nerve——!' she began furiously, and then from inside the flat there was the sound of a door opening, and her father's voice called irritably, 'Is that you, Lin?'

For the second time she saw the complete blankness of shock on Soren's face. But in a flash the look changed to one of sudden, cruel comprehension. It was a complication that she hadn't bargained on, and suddenly everything was too much for her to cope with. A nightmare of explanations and recriminations loomed, and she just shut her eyes and whispered fiercely, 'Oh, for God's sake, will you please just go away!'

When she opened her eyes again, her father was standing in the doorway and Soren was gone. Her father asked, 'What are you standing there for? Did I hear you talking to someone?' And she explained automatically that her car had broken down and someone from the party had given her a lift home. She heard the sound of Soren's car driving off fast, as her father urged her inside and shut the door.

Her car was standing on the road outside when she looked out the window after breakfast. Soren must have got up very early. There was no sign of him when she went out, and the car was locked, but after a moment's thought she looked in the letterbox at the gateway and found the keys there.

She didn't suppose she would ever see Soren again, and the thought should have brought some measure of relief, but all she could feel was a fierce pain succeeded by a hollow ache in her chest.

Somehow she got through the day, and her father didn't seem to notice anything amiss with her. In the afternoon he went out for a game of golf, which he played, apparently, quite well. He had never invited her to accompany him, and once when she had tentatively suggested that she might come along to watch, he stared at her for a few moments and then said shortly that she wouldn't enjoy it.

Lin went for a long walk, although the day was overcast, and odd spiteful little spurts of rain occasionally flung out of the looming clouds. She arrived home after her father, who seemed to disapprove of her walking in the rain, and she said lightly, 'Well, you played golf in it, didn't you?'

'That's not just aimless walking,' he said. 'You had no need to go out in the rain.'

Lin smiled a little sadly. She didn't remind him that he had no need to play golf, either, but she dimly saw that even his leisure pursuits, such as they were, must have some goal, something to be won, even if they were only games.

He said suddenly, 'Who brought you home last night?'

'Just someone else who happened to be at the party,' she shrugged.

'Someone you knew?'

'I—had met him before,' she said warily, taken aback by the unusual interest he was showing. He rarely questioned her about her friends.

She was even more surprised when he said, 'You don't have a boy-friend, do you?'

Cautiously, she replied, 'Not really—at the moment.'

He was frowning at her as though she presented something of a puzzle to him. 'You're twenty-four, aren't you?' He waited for her nod of agreement, then asked, 'Aren't most of your friends married?'

'I suppose so.' She didn't really have a lot of friends, and she had lost touch with most of the girls she had gone to school with.

'You're quite a nice-looking girl,' he said, his tone consciously kind. 'Haven't you had any proposals?'

Astonished, she said, 'I have, actually.' But none that she could have taken seriously. 'But I turned them down. Are you afraid I'll be left on the shelf?'

That was funny, and she laughed a little, because it was such a Victorian notion.

But her father didn't laugh. He looked vaguely irritated, and said, 'Well, you're surely not planning to stay—unmarried for ever, are you?'

Lin blinked and drew in a sharp breath. He had been going to say, *surely you're not planning to stay here for ever*. And then he had thought better of it, and gulped and hesitated on the word in mid-sentence before substituting the word *unmarried*.

She was still trying to assimilate that when he said abruptly, 'As a matter of fact, I'm thinking of getting married again myself.'

It shouldn't have been a bombshell, she supposed, but it was. So far as she knew her father had shown no interest in women since his wife's death. But then he shared so little of himself with her, he could easily have had a sort of secret life of which she was entirely ignorant.

Lin sank down on one of the expensive lounge chairs and said, 'S-someone in particular?'

'Of course someone in particular!' he snapped. 'My secretary—Miss Oxford. You know her.'

Lin fought a sudden desire to laugh. Poor pathetic Miss Oxford had finally brought it off, then. And her father had decided that such a treasure of a secretary should be permanently annexed. Not that there was anything funny, really, about middle-aged people getting married, or even falling in love. It happened all the time and Lin thoroughly approved. But she found it very difficult to imagine her father's secretary as a blushing bride, and even more so to see her father in the role of a lover.

'Wh-what's her first name?' she asked, and her father said, tersely, 'Bertha.'

It had a sweet old-fashioned ring, and Lin said, 'That's nice.' It also made Miss Oxford seem more human, and Lin felt a pang of pity for her, because she didn't think her father was going to be the easiest of husbands. Still, they said secretaries sometimes knew their bosses better than wives, so presumably she was going into this with her eyes open. Suddenly aware of the conventions, she said, 'Congratulations. Have you decided on a wedding date?'

'Not yet. There's no hurry,' he said, looking oddly embarrassed.

It took Lin a minute to work out the reason for the embarrassment—not bashfulness, but something else that chilled her. He wanted her out of his home before he brought his new wife into it. But he didn't want to have to say so outright.

A great wave of self-pity threatened to engulf her, but she pushed it back with grim determination. She wasn't a child, and a newly married couple certainly didn't want a grown-up daughter about, that was perfectly natural.

'I'd better find myself another flat,' she said.

'There's no hurry,' he muttered again, but she had seen the fleeting look of relief on his face, and she felt sick. 'If you need help with the rent——' he began. 'I mean, get yourself a nice place, my dear, and don't worry too much about the cost.'

With a sudden, shocking rush of contempt, she thought, Supposing I got myself a real luxury apartment, Daddy dear, would you pay up to get rid of me? Because that was what he wanted, to discharge his obligations, so far as she was concerned, preferably with money rather than with inconvenient intangibles like time and love. Because she wasn't his dear and never had been. And she had to remind herself that really it wasn't his fault.

It wasn't until nearly lunchtime the next day that Lin remembered she had promised to meet Susan. Tempted to skip the date, she thrust the idea from her. She couldn't do that to Susan, it wouldn't be fair. The friendship would have to be ended, and soon, but she could do it less unkindly than that.

It had been raining in the morning, but now the sun shone on wet pavements as she hurried towards their usual meeting place at the park. Every so often a gust of wind blew coldly as a cloud scudded over the sun, but the trees dripping over the narrow path looked washed and shining, and the colours of the autumn leaves scattered over the grass were brightened by the rain.

Lin shivered and put her head down against a brief, chill breeze as she drew near, then lifted her eyes to look for Susan. She saw Soren striding towards her, and stopped dead.

A moment later her instinct took over and she turned to walk quickly away. But the path was steep and strewn with slippery leaves, too dangerous to run on, and when she felt the inevitable hand close on her arm, she just stood rock-still and without looking at him said, 'I came to meet Susan.'

'I know,' he said. 'I came to meet you. Susan sends her apologies.'

Without much hope, she said, 'It was kind of you to bring the message. She isn't sick, is she?'

'No.'

He didn't elaborate, and after a moment she said, 'Well, thank you. Can I go now?' She glanced down pointedly at his hand still holding her arm.

'I'll buy you lunch.'

'No, thanks——'

'Oh, for God's sake stop fighting me,' he said wearily.

But Lin was stubborn. 'I'm not hungry, thanks.'

'Then you can watch me eat. I am.' He turned her and began walking her down the path, and with his hand urging her on she had no choice but to accompany him or create a stir by struggling and screaming.

She could have done that, she supposed, but the influence of civilisation was stronger in her than in him, so instead she said sarcastically, 'I'm sure it's a great honour to watch you eat, but I wish you'd confer it on some other lucky girl. Why don't you ask Rhoda to lunch, if you're lonely?'

'Why should I ask Rhoda?'

'For one thing, she's beautiful. And she—likes you.'

Callously, he said, 'She also talks too much. She never stops.'

Perversely, Lin leaped to the other girl's defence. 'She's a very nice girl!' she said hotly. 'And you'd be lucky if she looked twice at you—she could take her pick, she really could!'

He looked at her with an odd, fed-up expression as they descended a short flight of steps to the street. 'I know that,' he said. 'And for the record, she *has* looked twice at me. And had second thoughts, too. She's decided I scare her.'

Glancing up, Lin saw a faint grin on his mouth, and she said, 'Oh—did you try your caveman tactics on her, too?'

His quick return glance was amused. 'I didn't need caveman tactics with Rhoda. She's a sweet biddable creature. She apparently thinks of me as an intellectual scientist— and intellectual men make her nervous. But she hopes we'll always be friends.'

Slightly stunned, Lin said, 'She *said* that?'

'Rhoda says everything that comes into her head,' Soren told her dryly, as he steered her into the first coffee bar they came to, and thrust her into a seat. The seats all had high backs making each table into a semi-private booth. He stood looking down at her and said, 'Save my seat for me. Do you want coffee?'

She might as well, she supposed, so she said yes, and when he came back with a tray it held two steaming cups, and plates loaded with sandwiches, savouries and two slices of cheesecake.

'I got some extra in case you changed your mind,' he said, as he slid into the seat opposite.

Lin took an empty plate from the tray and put a sandwich on it, because although he had said he was hungry, he wasn't eating, and perhaps he was being polite and waiting for her to start.

But he went on stirring his coffee, looking down into the cup, and to break the silence, she said, 'Thank you for returning my car.'

He looked up, then, and said deliberately, 'I take it you found the keys all right. Is your—flatmate the man who gave you the car?'

Feeling her way, she said cautiously, 'Yes, actually. But——'

'And this?' He pushed back the sleeve of the jacket she wore and touched the gold watch on her wrist. 'And that pretty necklace you wore to the party—and the fur, of course.'

Lin's heart was beating hard and fast, but she clenched her teeth and said nothing.

Soren waited for a few moments, and then he said unemotionally, 'He's very generous.'

'He's very well off.' She had to say something, and that at least gave nothing away. She could see, of course, quite clearly, the way Soren's mind was working, and one part of her wanted to blurt out the truth; but a more sombre voice whispered, *Wait*.

'And you told Teresa you'd never been well off,' he said.

She looked up quickly, then, and he was looking at her with bitterness about his mouth, his eyes strangely distant, as though he was a long way from her. 'It puzzled me when she mentioned it,' he told her. 'Lot's of things about you puzzled me from the start. You had all the outward signs of—a certain affluence. And taking that job didn't fit in with that. In fact, nothing about you added up. You seemed anxious to become a part of the family and took an interest in all our affairs, and yet you obviously had secrets of your own, that nobody was allowed to hear. And when you got over loathing me, and began falling in love, you backed off and finally ran away.'

'I—never said I was in love with you. I made you no promises.'

'No. You were keeping your options open, weren't you?'

'What does that mean?'

'It means, I suppose, that I've been a fool. I kept thinking of rational explanations for all the contradictions, even for the lack of communication after you moved back to Auckland. When I heard via letters from home that you and Susan were seeing each other, I thought I'd get in touch and maybe you would explain a few things. I came up to see her and asked her where you live, but she didn't know. She didn't even know where you work. I could think of reasons why you wouldn't answer the phone to my mother, why you never took Susan to your home, why you wouldn't even tell her where you work. I didn't like any of them. But I wanted you to give me reasons, I thought maybe there was some I hadn't thought of.'

He paused, and Lin knew he was waiting, giving her the chance to give him the explanations he had hoped for. But she couldn't tell him the truth, and she wouldn't lie.

The silence lengthened, and she heard him let out a breath, as though he had been holding it. His voice sounded harsh as he went on: 'I can think of only one reason for the lie you told me the other night, when you said your flatmate was a she. How you live and who you live with is your own business, Melinda. But if you have to lie about it, that means you're ashamed.'

He let that sink in, and she wanted to protest, but the inner voice said, *Leave it, it's best this way. This will end it as nothing else could.*

Soren said, 'You're not in love with him.'

Lin looked down at her cooling coffee, saying nothing. And he repeated in a hard voice, 'You're not in love with him, *are you*?'

'I'm very fond of him,' she muttered, thinking it was the truth, but even as the words left her lips she wondered if it was.

'Were you living with him before you came to us?' he asked.

She hesitated, but the truth could do no more damage now. She said, 'Yes.'

'Did you have a quarrel? Or were you trying to break away?'

'I just wanted a change—for a while.'

She didn't look up to see his reaction to that.

His voice was cutting as he asked, 'Why—does he bore you?'

She gave a faint, bitter smile, because her father didn't bore her, but she knew very well she bored him.

'Was I too slow off the mark?' asked Soren. 'Maybe you hoped for a quick, sizzling affair before you returned to your elderly lover.'

'Elderly?' She looked up quickly, and his expression was cynical and decidedly unpleasant.

'I got a glimpse of him on Saturday night,' Soren explained. 'He is much older than you, isn't he?'

'Not elderly,' she said. 'Middle-aged, perhaps.'

'Is he married?'

Briefly, she felt fiercely angry. Did he really think she would live with a married man? Coldly, she looked straight at him, and said, 'He has been married.'

His eyes had the assessing look she had come to know. He said, 'And were you mixed up in his divorce?'

She could tell him there had been no divorce, but the

spurt of anger settled into a slow, smouldering flame, and she said, still meeting his eyes defiantly, 'No.'

'Are you hoping he'll make you his second wife?' Soren asked softly.

Lin had a sudden sense of *déjà vu*, and she realised that the tension weaving between them had the electric quality of their first encounters. Back then, he had angered her and she had thought she hated him, and she wanted to lash out now as she had then.

She smiled with conscious malice and said, 'It's funny you should say that. Only yesterday he said he was thinking of getting married again.'

For just a moment something flickered in his eyes, and she felt a tiny surge of triumph.

Then he said, 'Supposing I asked you to leave him, and marry me, Melinda. What would you say?'

She sat staring, conscious that every vestige of colour must have left her face. It felt cold and drawn. She could see nothing in his expression but a sort of deliberate, academic curiosity, and his eyes were penetrating but unreadable.

For a mad, mindless moment she was tempted to say yes, and let the future take care of itself. If he had said he loved her, if he had looked as though he meant it, she might not have had the will power to refuse. But his manner was chilling, and as she paused to consider if he meant it, or was playing some cruel, clever game of his own, sanity returned.

Without a tremor, she said tonelessly, 'The answer would have to be no.'

He didn't move, but his mouth smiled in a way that made her want to recoil from him. 'It was what I expected,' he said. Then he leaned back a little, and his eyes flickered over her. 'Well,' he drawled, 'perhaps it isn't too late for that brief, sizzling affair, before you tie the knot. I'd be happy to oblige, now that I know the score.'

Fury exploded in her brain. She felt her cheeks burn with humiliation and anger, and she spoke in a low, shaking voice. '*How dare you!*'

She rose to her feet in one swift movement, but Soren stayed where he was, his head tipped back, watching her with a derisive smile on his chiselled mouth. 'That's a very hackneyed exit line,' he drawled.

It was, but it expressed exactly how she felt, and she didn't see anything funny about it. She gathered up her bag from the seat, hating him for the pointed way he stayed lounging in his seat, knowing Teresa had taught him better manners than that, and that he was deliberately underlining his complete lack of respect for her as a woman.

She turned to go, and he said, with quiet force, 'Just a moment.'

She turned to look at him, and at last he got slowly to his feet, and he had stopped smiling. He had the look of a matador about to deliver the *coup de grâce*, and Lin braced herself in anticipation. Yet when the thrust came, she found she was unprepared for it. He said, 'I don't think you're a suitable friend for my young sister. I gather you've been kind to her, but you needn't trouble yourself any longer. I'll explain that you want nothing more to do with the Wingards. And you'll oblige me by not seeing her again.'

'*You can't*——!' she cried, and several people looked up curiously from their lunch. More quietly, she said, 'Soren, *please*——' She was begging him, but she didn't care. It wasn't fair for him to revenge himself on her by hurting Susan. 'Please——' she repeated. 'I'll put an end to our friendship, I promise you. But let me do it gradually, so she won't be hurt. At least let me do that for her——'

There was a frown in his eyes, but he seemed to consider what she had said, and finally he gave her a curt nod. 'All right, do it your way.' Then he added abruptly, 'You're genuinely fond of her, aren't you?'

'Yes,' she said simply. 'Thank you.'

They moved away from the table, and a couple of students looking for a table, with a tray holding yoghurt and fruit juices, asked Soren, 'You finished?'

He said, 'Yes,' and as they looked enquiringly at the untouched food and cold coffee on the table, he added curtly, 'You're welcome to it.'

'Well, at least you've brightened somebody's day,' Lin told him as they emerged into the street. Someone jostled her and apologised, and Soren took her arm to move her over near a shop doorway, out of the traffic. She said, 'I won't thank you for the lunch, because I didn't have any, but it's the thought that counts, isn't it?'

She was babbling and she knew it, and she was glad when he stopped her with a quietly forceful, 'Shut up!'

'Sorry,' she said. 'I suppose I sound like Rhoda.' Well, there were worse things. At least Rhoda wasn't a scarlet woman, like Melinda Blake. 'You could do worse than marry Rhoda, you know,' she said aloud.

Savagely, he repeated, 'I said, *shut up.*'

But she couldn't, because if she did she was going to burst into tears right here in the middle of the lunchtime rush hour, and worse, in front of him. She gave him a provocative smile instead, and said, 'You'll have to change your technique, though. I'm not surprised you scare her.'

Soren made a sound of suppressed fury and then, pushing her impatiently further into the doorway, he gripped her shoulders in his hands and muttered between his teeth, again, '*Shut up!*'

She thought he was going to shake her, but right in the middle of the lunchtime rush, he kissed her, in the most extraordinary way, hard, hungry and hurtful.

Someone going by laughed, and Soren let her go rather suddenly. Lin almost fell against the shop window behind her, and she put up a hand, and felt the knuckles bang against the glass.

She straightened herself with an effort and said, 'Wouldn't it be better if we just said goodbye like two civilised people? This isn't exactly the place for a big fare-well scene, is it? I did try to avoid having one remember?'

'I remember,' he said. He was breathing hard, and there was a faint line of dark colour along his cheekbones. She was suddenly shaken with compassion and helpless love for him, and her heart cried out against what they were doing to each other.

'I must go,' she said. 'I'll be late back at work. Don't come with me. Please, don't——'

And then she fled into the crowds on the footpath and didn't look back until she had passed the corner of the street. Soren wasn't in sight, and if he had followed her he would not have been far behind. They hadn't even said goodbye, she thought foolishly. Her foot turned on an un-even patch of the footpath, and she stumbled. A man reached out a hand to steady her, and saw the quick tears that had come into her eyes. He peered at her and said with concern, 'Are you all right?'

She could have said, *I think I'm dying, I feel as though I'm dying inside.* But she gave the man an unsteady smile and told him she was fine. She had ricked her ankle and it hurt a bit, that was all. He stayed by her a few paces and saw that she was walking without a limp, then he smiled and went on his way. That was kind of him, she thought with detachment. When Soren had caught her that first time they met, he hadn't stayed around to see if she was all right.

But Soren would have married her, even though she was another man's mistress.

Or—would he? He had asked her what she would say if he proposed, and she had said the answer would have to be no. She would never know if he would seriously have asked her to marry him. And suddenly that seemed worse than all the rest—the fact that she never would know.

CHAPTER TEN

Lin had a phone call later in the week from Susan, and arranged to meet her the following Saturday evening to go to a film. Lin asked if Rhoda might like to come, and was relieved when Susan said the other girl had a date already. Lin liked Rhoda, but she could never see her without remembering how wistfully she had looked at Soren the night of Lin's birthday party, and that memory brought others flooding back that at the moment she felt much to raw to cope with.

She couldn't help asking Susan casually, when she met her, if Rhoda's date was anyone she knew. If it was Soren she was inviting further pain, but the aching need to know what he was doing, who he was seeing, was overwhelming. It was another good reason to stop seeing Susan as soon as possible, of course. The wound was never going to heal if she kept on deliberately probing it like this.

But Susan said gaily, 'Oh, it's that advertising guy who was at the party—remember, he's got a curly beard and he had an orange tie.'

He sounded distinctive enough, and she should have remembered him, obviously, but Lin could recall very little of the party except that Soren had been there. She smiled vaguely and said, 'Oh, yes,' then led the way into the theatre.

When she dropped Susan off the younger girl asked, 'How about lunch on Monday?' Then she took a deep breath and said,

'Look, I'm going to be pretty tied up at work this week,

Susan. Could we make it the following week? Give me a ring then, and we'll make a day.'

'Okay.' The fact that she accepted that so cheerfully was an indication of her lessening reliance on Lin. It shouldn't be too difficult to wean her, now that she had Rhoda, and the flat would allow her to entertain her own university friends. She would probably scarcely notice when Lin quietly slid out of her life for ever. Only Lin felt a hollow heartache at the thought of it.

She had started looking for a place to live. It wasn't too easy because, in spite of his offer, she didn't want to use her father's money, and the price of accommodation, like everything else, was climbing every week. Then one of the girls at work mentioned that one of her three flatmates was moving out of the old house they shared in Ponsonby, and Lin went with her to see the room that night after work. It was large and she would have it to herself, although the bathroom was shared by the four of them. The kitchen facilities were unimaginative but adequately updated, and most important, the other girls seemed pleasant and quiet.

Her father looked doubtful when she told him where it was, but she reminded him that Ponsonby was becoming one of the trendier places to live, and many of the streets that had undoubtedly seen better days were now being facelifted and given a new lease of life. Anyway, it was only two minutes from the heart of the city by car, which certainly gave it an advantage over the outer suburbs.

It would be two weeks before the room would become vacant, but she told her father she had decided to take it, and gave him the date when she would be moving out. And she couldn't fool herself that there wasn't a certain satisfaction in his smile, even though he said, 'Well, my dear, I told you there was no hurry.'

Miss Oxford came to dinner one night, smiling nervously at Lin and inviting her diffidently to 'Call me Bertha, if you like.' Lin did so, but she didn't find it easy, and when Miss Oxford and her father entered into a deep discussion of business affairs, she felt more relieved than left out. She did ask them before the evening was out if they had set a date for their wedding, and noticed that Miss Oxford actually blushed faintly as her father mentioned a Saturday in the following month. Her offer of help with the arrangements was firmly declined by her father, who said, 'We don't want any fuss. The ceremony will be in the register office, and I'll arrange a meal afterwards at a hotel for a few colleagues and Bertha's relatives.'

Since that sort of thing was usually delegated to his secretary, Lin wondered if poor Bertha would have to make the bookings for her own wedding reception. She hadn't heard anything about Bertha's relatives before, either, but apparently she had a sister living in Auckland with her husband, and another sister and a brother would be invited to travel from further south and attend the wedding.

'Will Aunt Vera and Uncle Bill be invited?' she asked.

'Yes, of course,' her father said. 'Make a list, will you, Bertha?'

It seemed to Lin it boded to be an odd marriage; she could see no difference in her father's manner to his fiancée from that he had used to his secretary for the last ten years. But possibly in private he was more affectionate. All the more reason for her to move out and give them the privacy they would need.

She had assumed that Soren had returned to Wellington, so when Susan mentioned over their next lunch together that he had been at the flat the previous evening, she looked up in surprise. 'How long is he here for?' she asked. 'I thought it was just a short visit.'

'Oh, another couple of weeks, I think,' Susan answered. 'By the way, did I tell you Mum wrote that she might be coming to Auckland for a few days?'

Lin whitened. 'No, you didn't,' she said. 'Look, I must fly, Susan. We've got a rush on at the office just now. I'll see you around——'

She daren't see Teresa. She would have to keep Susan, somehow, from bringing them together. She could make her imminent move an excuse, she thought. She would be too busy to see anyone, and when she next contacted Susan, Soren would be gone, and perhaps Teresa's visit would be over. She would tell her father that if anyone rang for her she didn't want her new address given, or her phone number. He might think it a little odd, but he took very little interest in her affairs, and he would probably approve her caution, anyway, since he had expressed some mild concern about her new accommodation.

On Friday night she had sorted all her possessions and packed her clothes into suitcases for removal to the house, leaving her room bare except for the things she would need in the morning. She emptied the last drawer, and carefully placed in a small box a handpainted scarf that was a memento of her mother, a stuffed toy dog that her mother had made for her, not very expertly, a few books that she had owned since she was a child and never had the heart to give away, an old chocolate box which she didn't open, but which she knew contained a hand-knitted baby jacket and bonnet that had never been worn, and a red-covered photograph album.

The box was a little too small, and when she laid the album on top of the rest, she couldn't quite close the cardboard flaps.

Picking up the album, she laid it on the dressing table and closed the box, taping it down. She could carry the album in a paper bag, or something. She would find one tomorrow morning.

The place was very quiet, in spite of the hum of traffic a few blocks away on the main road. Her father had said he would be late tonight, and she hoped he had taken Bertha out on the town, but more likely the poor woman was slaving away for him over the typewriter.

Lin stood up, stretching to ease a crick in her back, and idly turned some pages of the photograph album. It was ages since she had looked in it. Once it had been her greatest treasure, a heavenly balm when her spirit needed soothing. She smiled sadly, picked it up and went into the sitting room, curling up in one of the big chairs with the album on her lap.

On the first page, carefully centred, was a wedding picture of her parents. She dimly remembered her mother helping her to paste it in, when she had been given the album. Then there were baby photos of herself, some with her mother, and one of her father holding her gingerly and looking uncomfortable. There was a school photograph taken when she was a solemn five-year-old, and a fuzzy snap of her mother that she had taken herself and proudly entered in the book. All it showed, really, was a halo of fair hair, a smile and a blue dress. Her father had been dark, before his hair greyed and thinned, and there was a picture of him with Lin at about ten, which one of her cousins had taken, and which was the last she had entered into the book. There were still about a dozen snaps which she had meant to put in it some day, inserted loosely between the last page and the back cover.

She riffled back through the pages, pausing at the pictures of her mother, as she had always done, ever since her child's world had fallen apart when her mother went out of it. Trying to conjure memories, she hardly heard the doorbell until it rang a second time, then she got up reluctantly and with the album still in her hands, went to answer it.

She switched on the porch light, so that she could dimly see the shape of the visitor on the other side of the rippled glass. It was not very late, but she was alone, and she was faintly reassured to see that the caller was a woman.

She opened the door, and Teresa smiled at her a little diffidently and said, 'Hello, Lin. Could I come in for a while?'

'Teresa!' Pleasure and dismay battled within her, but good manners at least demanded that the pleasure should be shown and the dismay hidden. She opened the door wide and said, 'Of course. Come into the sitting room.'

Teresa followed her into the room, and a hint of surprise showed in her eyes as she took in the deep pile carpet, the luxurious chairs and the expensive fittings. It had all been decorator-designed and no expense spared, and Lin had never compared it before with the comfortable modesty of the Wingard farmhouse. But Teresa was smiling at her as she unbuttoned her coat, and Lin said honestly, as she smiled back, 'I'm so glad to see you!'

Teresa seemed to relax, and Lin realised she had been unsure of her welcome. That phone call, of course. Teresa must have heard her speaking to the operator, and recognised her voice.

The older woman slipped off the coat, and Lin started forward. 'I'm so sorry! Can I hang it up for you?'

'Oh, it's all right here,' said Teresa, and casually draped it over a chair. She looked enquiringly at Lin, who said hastily, 'Oh, please—do sit down.' She still clutched the red album to her with one hand, but the other she waved vaguely at the chair.

Teresa settled herself, and Lin still stood looking at her in a slightly bemused way. Teresa's mouth curved and her eyes crinkled at the corners in delicious humour, and she said, 'And now, Lin, dear, what *is* this ridiculous idea of Soren's that you're some kind of old man's floozie?'

It did cross Lin's mind that she must pretend it was true, but she looked at the laughter in Teresa's face and knew that she hadn't believed it for a moment, and *of course* it was a ridiculous idea. All the high drama of her last meeting with Soren was suddenly put into perspective, in the light of Teresa's commonsense disbelief. A bubble of pure relief and happiness suddenly burst inside her and she began to laugh.

Teresa's laughter joined hers, and Lin collapsed into the chair opposite, and went on giggling until she had to gasp for breath.

She wiped her eyes and looked up, and Teresa was smiling at her, still. The laughter had been a catharsis, and a certain latent sympathy at the back of Teresa's eyes seemed to indicate that she knew that. Quizzically, she said, 'He told me you'd admitted it, that there was no shadow of a doubt.'

'But *you* doubted it,' Lin said gratefully.

'Oh, Lin! *You*——?'

Quite seriously, Lin said, 'Thank you.'

'I knew you better than that, and Soren should have, too. Were you very angry with him?'

'I didn't really admit anything,' Lin said. 'I just didn't deny it.'

'Well, if you wanted to punish him for his sordid suspicions, I can tell you he's thoroughly miserable.'

Distressed, Lin said, 'Oh—no! It wasn't that!' But now she had destroyed her story, and she was going to have to tell Teresa *something*, she realised. Agitatedly she asked, 'Can I get you some coffee?'

She rose from the chair and made to put the forgotten album on the coffee table beside her as she did so. But her eyes were on Teresa, and she misjudged the distance, catching the edge of the table with the book, which fell to the floor open and face down, and the photographs that had been loose at the back cascaded out of it and fanned across the carpet.

Lin bent swiftly to pick it up, and Teresa went down on her knees and began gathering the scattered photographs. But with several of them in one hand, she suddenly stopped, staring at the topmost one, and Lin, who had tried to grab them first, put out her hand quickly to take the pile. Teresa retained her grip, and Lin's fingers fell away. She said, with a shaky laugh, 'Baby photos—they're all alike, aren't they?'

It wasn't a very good picture. The baby showed clearly enough, but the girl who held the baby had her face half turned from the camera, and a curtain of dark hair obscured most of her features.

Teresa said in a strange voice, 'It's you, isn't it?'

Lin opened her mouth to say *no*, but the lie wouldn't come, and then Teresa looked up at her with an odd kind of longing in her eyes, and Lin said, 'Yes.'

Teresa stood up and put the photographs on the table, all but the one that had arrested her attention, then she picked up her coat and dug in a capacious pocket for a bulky leather wallet-style purse.

Lin watched as she pulled out a small, dog-eared print and laid it down beside the other. Then she turned and gave Lin a lopsided, wavering smile and said softly, 'Snap!'

Lin didn't need to look again to see that the photographs were identical. Her vision wasn't clear, anyway, because her eyes were blurred with tears. She said huskily, 'Do you always carry that with you?'

Teresa's voice wasn't very steady, either. 'Always,' she said. 'For twenty-four years.'

Lin said softly, 'Oh——!' and Teresa gave her a misty smile and said, 'We mustn't cry.'

She put out her hand and Lin put hers into it and said, 'No, of course we mustn't.'

But of course they did, then they laughed again, softly and in a rather watery fashion, and Teresa took both of Lin's hands in hers and said, 'Oh, you have grown up beautifully, darling!'

'Thank you,' said Lin. 'I must be like my mother.'

'Oh, Lin! Can you ever forgive me?'

'For giving me life? That's not to forgive!'

'For giving you up. Everyone told me it was the best thing I could do for you, to let someone adopt you and care for you better than I could have done. It was even harder to be a single mother, then, than it is now. I wanted to do what was right, for you.'

'I know. I know that you weren't just avoiding responsibility. Not you. My mother—my adoptive mother—kept the photo for me, and the baby clothes you made. I still have them. My father gave them to me when I was fifteen. He told me she'd said I should have them when I was old enough.'

'She must have been a very nice person.'

'I think she was. I don't remember her well, but I know I missed her dreadfully.'

'And—your father? I had the impression, from what you told me before, that you weren't close to him.'

'No. I live with him now—although I'll be moving out tomorrow—but it was hard for him after my mother—his wife died. I don't think he ever really wanted children, you see. When he was left with me on his hands, he didn't know what to do, really. But my aunt—did her best.'

'Oh, Lin—we all did our best, and yet you haven't been very well done by, have you?'

'Oh, but I have. I've always had a good home, been looked after, and the years I had with my mother were happy.'

'That says volumes about the years that came after,' Teresa said wryly. 'Of course, you've been more fortunate than many children, but I wanted my child to be loved, more than anything.'

That was what Lin had wanted, too. 'I'm sure I was,' she said. She had never been certain of that, but she wanted Teresa to believe it. 'Shall we have that coffee?'

Teresa came into the kitchen with her, but they took the cups back to the sitting room because the heater was on there, and as they sipped it, Teresa asked, 'Did you know—when you came to us?'

'Yes. I wanted to know about my natural parents— especially my mother. About a year ago I began to try and find out. It was difficult, adoption records are supposed to be confidential, of course. The fact that you came from a small town helped, though. I was able to go through some of the records of births and marriages, and one social worker was quite helpful, although some others disapproved very much. I was warned time and again what it might do to you. And I never intended you to know. When I did finally trace you to Paikea, I didn't know what to do next. I wanted to just get one good look at you, somehow, without your knowing about it all. And then I saw the advertisement, and it was——'

'Providential?'

'Yes. I couldn't pass up the chance to get to know you. But I swore to myself I wouldn't alter anything, that you would never know.'

'Oh, Lin, didn't it ever occur to you that I might be

longing to know what had happened to my baby girl?'

'Yes. But that was a temptation, you see. I couldn't assume that. It might have been just wishful thinking on my part.'

'But after you got to know me—— Lin, it would have meant so much to me if you'd told me.'

'It wasn't my secret, and I couldn't be sure. You might not have wanted to be reminded. I didn't even know if you'd told Ray, and—and if I did say anything, you might have felt you had to tell him, then. I couldn't be responsible——'

'Heavens! Do you really think I could have married *anyone* and not told him a thing like that?'

'No. But I didn't dare trust my feelings, you see. They might have led me astray. I just had to keep to my original plan of leaving things just as they were.'

'My dear,' Teresa said gently, 'that wasn't possible.'

'No. I'm sorry, I didn't mean to cause trouble.'

'Soren——'

'Your son,' Lin said softly.

'Yes. Do you mind that?'

'I did, at first. I was jealous. And then——'

'Then you loved him. But you left because you'd made some silly vow about leaving things as you found them.'

Lin's smile was a trifle pale. 'It wasn't so silly,' she said. 'You must see that I can't marry Soren.'

'Can't you? Why not?'

'Because—because he might find out that—that you——'

'That I had an illegitimate baby twenty-four years ago?'

'Teresa, you know how he feels about you. He nearly worships you! I can't marry him and keep a secret like that from him, and he can't be allowed to find out.'

'*That's* why you turned him down?' Teresa said slowly. 'Because you're afraid of shattering his image of me?'

'You do understand?' Lin pleaded.

'I understand. And I've never heard such nonsense in all my life! Oh, I know he likes to think I belong on a pedestal, but I refuse to stay there just to satisfy his sense of—of propriety! It's high time that young man learned to see women for what they are, not what he thinks they are, or ought to be! I think I shall just inform him of the facts of life!'

Looking rather militant, Teresa rose to her feet, putting aside her coffee cup and picking up her coat.

Alarmed, Lin stood up, too. 'But, Teresa, you *can't* tell him! Think what it will do to him!'

'I hope it shakes him to the core!' Teresa said tartly. 'He has no judgment of women at all. Fancy him thinking my daughter was a mercenary little tart!'

She was buttoning her coat with quick fingers, and Lin said deprecatingly, 'I did give him cause, I suppose.'

'Rubbish! One look at you should have been enough to tell him you were never that kind of girl.'

'I don't think he trusts his own judgment——'

Interrupted by the sound of the outside door opening, Lin looked up as her father came into the room.

Bertha wasn't with him, but he was looking quite pleased with himself, and Lin surmised that the evening, whether it was work or romance, had gone well.

He looked questioningly at her visitor, and as Lin hesitated over the introduction, Teresa held out her hand and said, 'You must be Lin's father. I'm Teresa Wingard.'

'Oh, yes,' he said, after a moment. 'Lin—ah—worked for you in the Bay of Plenty.'

'That's right. I don't know what we'd have done without her.' Teresa smiled. 'She's a lovely girl. You must be proud of her.'

'Er—yes, I am,' he agreed vaguely, looking surprised.

Teresa looked at him thoughtfully and said, 'Well, I must be going. It's been nice meeting you, Mr Blake.'

Lin went with her to the door, murmuring anxiously, 'Teresa, do you really think you should——? Is Soren still in Auckland?'

And Teresa said firmly, 'Yes, I really think I should. And Soren is waiting for me.'

Lin gasped and said, *'Outside?'*

'No. He wanted to wait in the car, but I didn't fancy the thought of him prowling about out there while we talked, and I made him stay at his motel and promised I'd come back.'

'Did he—send you?'

'Sort of. He more or less challenged me to come and see for myself. He would never admit it, of course, but he was hoping I could talk you out of what he thought was your —your way of life.'

Still troubled, Lin asked, 'What do you think he'll do?'

Understanding her perfectly, Teresa smiled and said, 'I think he'll want to see you, straight away. Will you be here when he comes? I know it's late, but I don't think I'll be able to stop him.'

'I'll be here,' Lin promised. Her knees felt weak, though, and Teresa smiled at her reassuringly and kissed her cheek.

'Don't worry. I'd like to tell the world, but perhaps we'll just let the general public think I've acquired a particularly super daughter-in-law.'

'Will you mind if I call you Ma?' Lin asked, with a shaky smile.

'I'll love it!'

Lin closed the door after her and went slowly back to the sitting room. Her father was still standing in the middle of the room, frowning absently down at the carpet. 'She seems a pleasant woman,' he commented.

Lin wondered how he would react if she said, 'She's

my mother.' She smiled a little to herself, and touched the back of the chair in which Teresa had been sitting. 'They're a nice family,' she said. 'I think—I may marry her son.'

'Really?' For once she had captured his full attention. 'Has he asked you?'

'Yes,' she said. 'But I haven't given him an answer.' It wasn't quite true, of course, but it approximated the situation closely enough. Lin only hoped that Teresa wasn't wrong about Soren's probable reaction. He might feel so thoroughly disillusioned that he would turn into a complete woman-hater for the rest of his life.

'Well, that's very nice,' said her father, and then, apparently feeling the inadequacy of the words, he came over to her and put a clumsy arm about her shoulders and gave them a squeeze. 'Well, well,' he said. 'So my little girl is going to be married.' Then he stood holding her as. though he had got into a situation that he didn't quite know how to get out of. And Lin, with an odd little rush of affection mingled with pity for this man who had tried to be a good father, but never really got the hang of it, laughed a little and kissed his cheek and slipped away from his arm to pick up the coffee cups.

'Would you iike a cup of coffee, Dad?' she asked him.

'No, thanks, my dear. I think I'll get to bed. Are you staying up?'

'Yes. I think Soren—Soren Wingard—may be calling in later tonight.'

'Oh. That's—er—him?'

'That's him.' Lin grinned suddenly, and was surprised when her father smiled back at her, and for a moment they were closer than they had ever been, although half the width of the room was between them.

'Should I stay and ask him about his intentions?' he asked unexpectedly.

Lin laughed delightedly. Really, this was turning into a most extraordinary evening! 'I don't think so,' she said. 'You can do that another time, but I'd like to give him my answer first.'

'All right, my dear. I shall look forward to meeting him. What *are* his prospects, by the way? I know it's quite proper for you not to care, but it's my duty to see that you're provided for, you know.'

Tonight, she didn't even care about that word *duty*. In the last few minutes their relationship had subtly shifted, and although it would never be perfect, it might become something unique and precious to them both, if it was carefully nurtured.

She answered him gaily, 'I expect they're quite good, really,' and she told him what Soren did. He was approving and even mildly impressed. Lin was glad, because she would have married Soren anyway, but it was nice that her father could approve.

When her father had gone to bed, she washed the cups, humming quietly, then she went into her own room and inspected herself in the mirror. Her eyes were softly shining, and although there were faint shadows beneath them because she hadn't slept well lately, her cheeks had a healthy flush of colour tonight.

She stripped off the jeans and shirt she had been wearing, and put on a pair of midnight blue velvet slacks with a long-sleeved powder blue blouse, knotting the front ends of the blouse at her waist. She used some eye make-up, smoothing blue shadow across her lids, and smeared a lip gloss over her mouth, blotting off the stickiness with a tissue, leaving the faintest hint of colour.

And then there was nothing to do but wait.

Perhaps he wouldn't come, after all. Perhaps Teresa had been horribly wrong, and he wanted nothing more to do with her. Lin brushed her hair again, unnecessarily, and tried to calm her jumping nerves.

And when the doorbell pealed, she sat utterly still and panic-stricken for long, breathless moments before she jumped up and flew to open the door.

She had wondered if he would arrive chastened, or grim, or gently loving. She opened the door and he was standing with the light behind him, but when he stepped into the hallway and pushed the door to behind him, she instinctively stepped backwards towards the sitting room, because what she had not expected was that he would come to her in a towering rage.

He followed her into the room, like a great animal stalking its prey, and slammed that door behind him, too, standing in front of it with his eyes blazing fury and his mouth hard.

Lin fell back another step when he moved slightly, and then she raised her chin and stood her ground, her heart thumping.

Soren's eyes narrowed a little and he almost smiled, but not nicely. 'You're scared of me,' he said.

Of course she was scared, he was a big man, and he didn't look in the least loving. She had never seen him so blazingly angry before.

But she faced him with defiance, her head thrown back, and her hands on the waistband of the velvet trousers, and said, with coolly raised brows, 'Should I be?'

His mouth scarcely moving, he replied, 'Yes, you should. Because I'm about ready to *strangle* you!'

Oh, God! she thought. Oh, Teresa, now we've done it! Teresa had been wrong, horribly wrong. Teresa had insisted on coming down from the pedestal Soren had made for her, and the revelation of her feet of clay had hurt. He

was hurt and he was angry and he knew it was all Lin's
fault.

She felt sick with disappointment, and a tearing hurt because *he* had been hurt, but under it all there stirred a rage
of her own. Because Teresa was a terrific person, no matter
that she wasn't the plaster saint he had made her out to
be in his own mind. And he had no right to be angry because she had tumbled from that ridiculous and unneces-
sary pedestal.

He moved, and she tensed and said quickly, 'My father's
here, and if you touch me I'll scream the place down!'

He grated, 'When has your father ever protected you?'
and kept coming.

And Lin, her inner rage exploding to the surface, hit
him with her open hand as hard as she could. Even as she
did it her mind was appalled at the action, but her hand
connected with all the weight of her arm behind it, and
Soren winced before his hands fell on her shoulders and
jerked her towards him, her eyes wide and her teeth on
her lower lip to stop a cry of pain.

Her hand pushed against his hard chest, and she felt
the hurried beating of his heart against her palm. She drew
in a breath and opened her lips to scream as she had
threatened, but the sound was strangled in her throat as
his mouth came down on hers in a long, hard, angry kiss.

She struggled, but couldn't find her balance, and she
tried to pull back her head, but his mouth didn't leave
hers, and she found her neck was unbearably stretched. Her
hands clutched at his shirt and she moaned a protest, and
he shifted his grip, gathering her into his arms, her body
arched against his, and her head pressed against the curve
of his arm. Then the quality of the kiss changed. The
violent anger abated, and a demanding passion took its

place, coaxing her bruised mouth into a reluctant sub-mission, and then to sweet response. Then Soren was sud-denly gentle, his fingers moving softly up her spine and caressing her nape, her cheek, and the skin behind her ear as his lips moved whisper-light on hers.

Her arms went up to hold him close to her, and she murmured his name against his mouth. He picked her up and took her the few steps to the long, wide sofa and sat with her cradled in his arms, her feet on the crushed velvet upholstery.

He shifted so that his shoulder was against the cushions at one end of the sofa, and when he lifted his mouth at last from hers, her head fell naturally against his shoulder. He smoothed her hair back from her temple and dropped a light kiss on it, and then his mouth trailed across the skin of her cheek to her jawline. Instinctively Lin moved her head, arching her neck for him, and smiling as his lips ex-plored it and his tongue found the beating little pulse in the hollow at its base. His hand stroked her waist and hip, and turning her face against the strong, warm column of his neck as he raised his head again, she said softly, 'Why were you so angry?'

'Was I angry?' he murmured, turning his head to kiss her eyelids.

She laughed and took his face in her hands, feeling the bones under the taut skin, and the slight abrasiveness of his shaven cheeks. 'You said you'd strangle me,' she re-minded him.

'I might do that yet,' he said, and caught her hands in his, turned the palms up within his, and kissed them. 'When I've finished with you.'

'That sounds ominous,' she said, looking lovingly into his green eyes. 'What are you planning to do with me?'

'Marry you,' he said, looking back at her with a lambent

flame in the green depths. 'And make love to you for ever.'

'Then you'll never be finished with me,' she said breathlessly.

'That's right, you may avoid strangulation, after all.' His fingers were on her throat, but they were thrilling, not threatening, touching her skin as though he loved the texture of it, and she said,

'You're not making sense.'

'Lovers don't have to make sense.'

She wasn't going to make sense if he kept stroking her the way he was doing, Lin thought, and she caught his wandering hand in hers and laid her cheek against his palm. 'Are you my lover?' she asked him.

'Yes. For the rest of our lives.'

'You haven't asked me to marry you,' she reminded him.

'You told me what you'd say if I did. I'm not taking the risk.'

She choked on silent laughter. 'Then how do you know I will?' she asked reasonably.

'You will.' He kissed her, parting her lips softly with his until her response couldn't have left any doubt of her answer. And when he had finished he laughed softly and repeated, 'You will.'

'Yes,' she admitted, 'I will.' She had her arms about his neck, and she put her forehead against the opening of his shirt and said, 'Did it upset you, what Teresa told you?'

'It stunned me,' he confessed.

'I'm sorry,' she said. 'I didn't want her to tell you.'

'So she said,' he drawled, and she lifted her head and looked at him, because she knew that tone, and it was ominous.

'You thought I couldn't take it,' he said, with a hardness in his eyes. 'What kind of neurotic oaf do you think I am?'

'I don't,' she said weakly. 'I was so afraid you'd be hurt ...'

'Hurt——? My God, do you think it didn't hurt when you tore my heart out and trampled on the pieces? Did you think that was better than letting me find out that the girl I was in love with was the daughter of the woman I've loved most in the world—until now?'

'I—d-didn't know you felt like that,' she stammered. 'I thought—you'd get over it. You never said you were in love with me.'

'You didn't give me the chance,' he told her. 'You went away, and I thought—that's another girl who didn't wait for me.'

'I felt it was the only thing to do,' she said soberly. 'I didn't have the right to love you. It all seemed so complicated, and I was so afraid of letting out Teresa's secret and causing trouble in the family. I had to protect her, and I—thought I was protecting you, too. You're not—disappointed in her now, are you?'

'How could I be? I've loved her and respected her since I was eleven years old, and nothing can change what she is to me. And besides that, she's given me you.'

'But you were so furious when you came in,' she said. 'You didn't have a row with Teresa, did you?'

'No. When I left her, I still wasn't sure what had hit me. But as I drove over here, it began to dawn on me that you'd nearly wrecked our lives with your idiotic scruples and evasions.' His hand gripped her shoulders and gave her a little shake. 'How dared you sit there and let me make such a monumental fool of myself—how could you let me believe all those things I hurled at you?'

'It seemed to me that, if you believed them, it would be easy for you not to love me. And I thought, maybe you wanted to believe them.'

'I *wanted* you to deny them!' he said forcefully. 'I was

hoping like hell that you would tell me that it was all un-true. I wouldn't even have asked for proof, if you'd just said it wasn't so!'

'Teresa knew it wasn't so, without being told,' said Lin.

He bent his head and rubbed his cheek against her temple. 'Yes. I know she did. She told me I had a warped view of women, and I guess she was right. I'm sorry, love, I've got a lot to learn.'

'I'll teach you,' she said, her lips touching his cheek with soft little kisses. 'To love—and trust—and believe in me.'

Soren began, 'Promise me——' then abruptly stopped, his lips clamped shut. And Lin knew he dared not ask for her promise.

She touched his fair hair with her fingers and kissed his mouth and said, 'I'll never leave you, Soren, never of my own will. And when you leave me, I'll wait for you, I promise.'

'I'll never let you go,' he said quietly. 'Never in this world.'

His lips found her mouth and then her throat, and she felt his hand on her rib cage, and moved it to her breast, holding its warmth against her. He murmured in her ear, 'Hussy!'

She smiled, and said dreamily, 'Not at all fit company for your sister. Am I?'

Soren moved abruptly, pushing back his hair as he sat up. 'Lord, don't remind me!' he muttered. 'It was a vicious thing to say to you.'

'Yes,' she said serenely. 'And I thought you Wingards didn't adhere to the old double standard?'

'Meaning?' he said tersely.

'Well, considering you'd just suggested that you and I should have a *brief, sizzling affair*, I did wonder after-wards if you would consider yourself any better company for Susan than I was?'

He looked at her with a hint of uncertainty, and she let the smile show in her eyes.

The green depths of his mirrored it, and he said, 'I'm glad you didn't think of it at the time. I don't know what I could have said, without making an even bigger fool of myself than I had already.'

'You weren't a fool,' she said. 'As a matter of fact, you were rather magnificent. Did you really mean it—about having an affair?'

He suddenly looked grim. 'I meant it. I would have taken you on any terms, hoping to persuade you into marriage.'

'I wasn't sure if you meant it, either, when you asked if I would marry you. I thought you might be playing some cruel joke.'

His face sombre, he said, 'It was no joke.'

'You really wanted to marry me, even though——'

'Even though,' he confirmed.

Lin said, 'You must love me very much.' Her voice shook; and Soren tightened his arm about her and said, 'Haven't I convinced you of that, yet?'

'Actions speak louder than words,' she said demurely.

'Is that so?'

He pushed her shoulders back against the cushions and held her there, pinning her with his eyes. 'Where is your father?' he asked her softly.

'In bed. He wants to see you tomorrow—to find out what your intentions are regarding his daughter.'

'That's tomorrow. You said you'd scream for him. If I touched you.'

His eyes roamed over her face and throat and slipped down over her body, and although he had moved his hands to the arm and back of the sofa, she shivered, because he was making love to her, and they both knew it.

'You're not touching me,' she whispered.

He leaned forward then, without moving his hands, then touched her lips with his, and said, 'Scream.'

She smiled against his mouth and murmured, 'Why? Am I in danger?'

He sat back a little and quirked an eyebrow at her. 'You don't think so?' he asked.

Lin shook her head. 'Not from you. Never from you.'

'No,' he said. 'I'll be your protector from now on. But you were scared of me tonight.'

'Only when I thought you'd stopped loving me. That's the only thing I could be scared of, now. I'd be very frightened, then—if you stopped loving me.'

'Then you have nothing in the world to be frightened of. Because that will never happen.'

'No, it never will,' she said with great confidence. She traced the shape of his face with her fingertips and placed them against his mouth, letting him kiss them. 'Is Teresa waiting for you?' she asked.

He took her hand in his and said, 'I left her at the motel, but she would have gone back to the girls' flat. She's staying with Susan and Rhoda. I bet she doesn't sleep a wink!'

'I was supposed to have an early night,' Lin told him. 'I'm moving out tomorrow.'

'Where to?' he asked with a quick frown.

She told him, and he said, 'Leaving no address, I suppose. I caught you just in time, didn't I?'

Shaken at the thought, she said, 'Yes. Tomorrow might have been too late.'

'Must you go there?' he asked. 'Leave your stuff packed, and we'll get married as soon as we possibly can. Then you can move into our new home instead.'

'Yes,' she said instantly. 'I'd like that.' She laughed suddenly. 'Tomorrow is going to be different from what I'd thought——'

'Better?' he queried.

'Infinitely better,' she said. 'Wonderful!'

For the first time in her life, she was greedily counting all the tomorrows that lay ahead of her. Some would bring happiness, and perhaps some might bring sorrow, but Soren would be there to share the happiness and make the sorrow bearable. And she would do the same for him. Oh, yes—tomorrow was something to look forward to.

Harlequin Romances

The books that let you escape
into the wonderful world of romance!
Trips to exotic places...interesting
plots...meeting memorable people...
the excitement of love.... These are
integral parts of Harlequin Romances –
the heartwarming novels read by
women everywhere.

Many early issues are now available.
Choose from this great selection!

Choose from this list of Harlequin Romance editions.*

*Some of these book were originally published under different titles.